The Elijah Project

Trapped by Shadows

Other Bill Myers Books You Will Enjoy

The Elijah Project
On The Run
The Enemy Closes In
Trapped by Shadows
The Chamber of Lies

The Forbidden Doors Series
The Dark Power Collection
The Invisible Terror Collection
The Deadly Loyalty Collection
The Ancient Forces Collection

Teen Nonfiction
The Dark Side of the Supernatural

The Elijah Project

Trapped by Shadows

Bill Myers

bestselling author

ZONDERkidz

ZONDERVAN.com/
AUTHORTRACKER
follow your favorite authors

For John Fornof:

A man of God who knows about fighting the good fight.

Zonderkidz

Trapped by Shadows
Copyright © 2009 by Bill Myers

Requests for information should be addressed to:
Zonderkidz, *Grand Rapids, Michigan* 49530

Library of Congress Cataloging-in-Publication Data

Myers, Bill, 1953-
    Trapped by shadows / by Bill Myers.
        p. cm. — (Elijah project ; bk. 3)
        Summary: When the forces of the evil Shadow Man kidnap six-year-old Elijah, his
    parents and siblings, Zach, aged sixteen, and Piper, aged thirteen, face their own weaknesses
    when they enter the Abyss to try and save him.
        ISBN 978-0-310-71195-7 (softcover)
        [1. Supernatural — Fiction. 2. Christian life — Fiction 3. Healing — Fiction. 4. Adventure
    and adventurers — Fiction. 5. Brothers and sisters — Fiction. 6. Angels — Fiction. 7.
    California — Fiction.] I. Title.
    PZ7.M98234Trd 2009
    [Fic] — dc22

                                                                            2008045730

Published in association with the literary agency of Alive Communications, Inc., 7680 Goddard Street #200, Colorado Springs CO 80920, www.alivecommunications.com.

Zonderkidz is a trademark of Zondervan.

Editor: Kathleen Kerr
Art direction: Merit Alderink
Cover illustration: Cliff Neilsen
Interior design: Carlos Eluterio Estrada

Printed in the United States of America

09 10 11 12 13 14 15 /DCI/ 9 8 7 6 5 4 3 2

Table of Contents

Therefore put on the full armor of God, so that when
the day of evil comes, you may be able to stand
your ground, and after you have done everything,
to stand.

—Ephesians 6:13

Chapter One

Pursuit

Thirteen minutes before midnight, three vehicles from three different directions sped toward a single destination, their occupants all focused on a single goal.

●

From the north, a mud-splattered Jeep Cherokee raced through the night. Dad concentrated harder as he tightened his grip on the wheel. His headlights caught a sign: Speed Limit 55. It whipped from sight as the Jeep slid around another curve.

"Mike!" his wife warned, her knuckles white as she clutched the dashboard.

"If we get pulled over, I'll explain our kids are in danger," said Dad, his mouth in a hard line as he stared ahead.

●

From the south, a sleek black Hummer roared down the highway. Its dashboard was lit up with indicators like the cockpit of a fighter jet: digital readouts, GPS map, radar screen, infrared monitor, and a flashing red light from the tracking device that had been attached to the underside of the mud-splattered Jeep, now only a few short miles away.

The glow from the dash lit the driver's face. He glanced into his rearview mirror, caring not so much what was on the road behind him so much as what was in the seat behind him — a dark presence that soaked up all the light around it.

Shadow Man.

●

And from the west, lumbering along as fast as it could, was an old beat-up RV camper. Its worn engine coughed and choked, puffing blue smoke out of its tailpipe.

Inside, sixteen-year-old Zach held the steering wheel with one hand while stuffing his mouth with the other — a Super Extreme Nuclear Burrito, featuring Flaming Fire Fajita Chicken. And forget the wimpy hot or extra hot sauce. Not for Zach. He'd gone for Taco Wonderland's newest sauce, the kind they advertised as *Danger: Explosive!*

Behind him, in the back of the RV, sat his thirteen-year-old sister, Piper. As the ultra-responsible one of the group (someone had to be), she was taking care of their six-year-old brother, Elijah.

"All right," she said, carefully tapping out some raisins into the little boy's hand, "you can have eight now and eight more when we get there."

Elijah, who hardly ever spoke, looked up at her with his big brown eyes and smiled—his way of saying thank you.

She smiled back. "Don't worry, it won't be long before we see Mom and Dad again. I promise."

Elijah nodded and laid his head on her arm. Piper tenderly stroked his hair, hoping she was right. Without her mom there, the job of caring for the little guy fell into her hands. Which was okay. She loved Elijah. He could be so sweet and caring ... when he wasn't being so weird. Honestly, she'd never met anybody like him. Sometimes it was like he knew what was going to happen before it happened. Sometimes when he visited sick people, they were suddenly well. And sometimes when the family really, absolutely needed something to happen, she'd see his little lips moving in prayer, and, just like that, it happened. Not all the time. But just enough to make things a little freaky.

And speaking of freaky, there was her older brother, Zach—it wasn't just his eating habits that were adventurous. It was everything he did. From seeing how fast a skateboard could go if you attached rocket motors to it (answer: ninety-three miles an hour before he crashed into a tree, flew through the air, and landed in someone's kiddie pool), to seeing how many bottles of ketchup you could drink before your hurl (answer: 1½), to talking his littler sister (as in Piper) into sticking her tongue on the frozen monkey bars in the middle of winter to see what would happen (answer: a visit by the paramedics who had to pour hot water on her tongue to unfreeze it from the bars).

Good ol' Zach. That's why she had to keep an eye on him all the time. Like now, when she looked up front and spotted him biting into his burrito. Like now, when his eyeballs bulged and his dark hair—which usually looked like it was styled by a fourteen-speed blender stuck on Super Chop—seemed to stand on end.

She could tell he wanted to say something. She could also tell that his mouth was on fire. Which explains why the only word that came out was:

"AAAAAAAAAAAAAAH!"

"What's wrong?" Piper shouted. Then she saw the wrapper on the floor and understood. "Nuclear burrito?"

Zach nodded, waving air into his mouth, which caused the RV to swerve from side to side.

Piper sprang for the RV's sink. She turned the water on full blast and yanked up the sprayer, pulling the long hose to the driver's seat.

The RV bounced onto the road's shoulder as Zach slammed on the brakes, finally bringing the vehicle to a skidding stop.

"Open your mouth!" she yelled.

He obeyed.

She aimed for the screaming hole in Zach's face and pressed the sprayer.

The water hit its mark, and Zach's mouth sizzled like a frying pan dumped in cold water.

●

Meanwhile, in the Jeep, all Dad could think of was getting to his children before the other side did. He'd seen the evil their leader could do and he didn't like it. Not one bit. He wasn't sure if those dark powers came from this world or from somewhere else. Either way, the children had to be protected.

●

In the Hummer, the driver focused on the tracker beam and the GPS map. This time there would be no mistakes.

●

And in the RV, Zach's mouth continued to smolder.

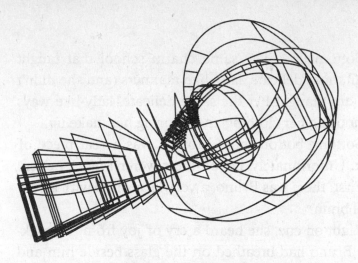

Chapter Two

The Plot Sickens

There was a fourth vehicle: a dark green van sitting on the shoulder of the highway.

Inside, Monica Specter's red, shaggy hair shone in the mirror light. She was busy applying another layer of bright red lipstick and shimmering, electric-green eye shadow. Granted, sometimes in the bright sunlight all that makeup made her look a little bit like a clown. But in this dimmer light she looked more like a ... well, all right, she still looked like a clown.

And don't even ask about her clothes. More often than not, it looked like somebody had just stitched a bunch of bright beach towels and bedspreads together and thrown them on her. It's not that she didn't have any fashion sense. It's just that ... well, all right, she didn't have fashion sense either.

Bottom line: The same charm school that taught her all those delicate, lady-like manners (and she didn't have any) taught her the same delicate, lady-like ways of choosing her clothing and wearing her make up.

Bottom, bottom line: Monica was a real piece of work. Unfortunately, her partners weren't much better:

First, there was Bruno, a very large man with a very small brain.

Right on cue, she heard a cry of joy from the back-seat. Bruno had breathed on the glass beside him and fogged it up. He drew a smiley face with his finger ... to join an entire family of smiley faces he'd drawn across the window. "Wanna see me do it again?"

Then there was Silas, a pointy-nosed, pointy-chinned, pointy-everything guy with bloodshot eyes and big, droopy bags under them the size of hammocks.

"Not again ..." Silas sighed. "I don't ever want to see another smiley face in my life. Do you understand?"

Bruno paused in deep thought. "So ... you want me to draw little frowny faces, instead?"

Silas turned away and moaned.

"Will you two grow up?" Monica snarled from the front seat. (Snarling was one of her specialties.)

"I'm not the one who needs to grow up," Silas argued. "He is." He thrust a pointy thumb in the direction of his partner.

"No sir," Bruno said. "You are!"

"No, you are!"

"Liar, liar, pants on—"

"Knock it off!" Monica shouted. "You're acting like big, fat, stupid morons!"

Bruno sucked in his gut. "I'm not fat."

Monica could only stare. They had been sitting here

on the side of the road for hours, waiting for the kids' RV to rumble past. And they were definitely going stir-crazy.

But Monica was as determined as she was nasty. This time she would not fail. Shadow Man wanted the little boy. He never said why, but there was something very, very valuable about him. And she would deliver him. She had to. This was her chance to finally prove her worthiness.

She glanced at her two partners sulking in the backseat. They'd been assigned to her since the beginning — a skinny little weasel and a brainless baboon. They had bungled every assignment she'd been given.

But this time, it would be different.

Headlights suddenly appeared in the mirror.

"Duck!" she called back to them. "Duck!"

Bruno's face brightened. "You want me to draw a duck?"

"Duck! Duck!" she cried.

"Goose!" Bruno shouted back in glee.

"No, you moron," Silas scooted down in the seat. "She means *get down!*"

Silas yanked him down in the seat just as the RV swooshed by, rocking the van in its wake. Once it had passed, Monica rose and turned on the ignition. The van's engine roared to life. This time, the kid would be hers.

●

To anyone else, the run-down garage was packed with yesterday's junk. The sagging shelves bulged with old televisions, radios, and out-of-date computers. But to the inventor's eye, these old gadgets and circuit boards were the building blocks of imagination.

Willard, a pudgy genius with curly hair, punched in

numbers on his laptop. His reluctant assistant, Cody, watched with concern.

It was getting late, and they had to hurry.

"One more calculation ..." Willard punched a key on the laptop keyboard with the flair of a concert pianist hitting the last note of a great concerto, " ... and the program has now reached terminal status!"

Cody, who was definitely smart but not "Willard smart," turned to him and in his most intelligent voice asked, "Huh?"

"We're done!"

"Why didn't you just say 'we're done'?"

"I am a man of science," replied Willard, closing the laptop with a flourish.

"No, you're a guy who uses big words."

"Oh," Willard nodded knowingly. "You mean a *logophile*. Or a *logogogue*. Or possibly a *logomachist*. Or—"

"Willard?"

"Yes, Cody?"

"Be quiet."

Willard grinned as the laptop's lights flickered greenly. "I will gladly desist, my friend."

Cody started to answer, then stopped. Willard had always been smart. But lately he'd been testing his vocabulary ... and Cody's patience. A lot of people get their exercise by working out with weights. Willard worked out with words. Not that Cody blamed him. At school everyone made fun of him. Maybe this was his new way of fighting back.

Cody continued watching. "You still haven't told me how these are going to help Piper and her family."

"It will momentarily become clear," Willard said. "And you shall have nothing further to worry about."

Cody sighed, running his fingers through his hair. He'd heard that before. "That's what worries me."

"Here." Willard handed him two leg harnesses. "Put these on. They will assist in the stabilization process."

As Cody grabbed the leg harnesses, he thought back to some other not-so-successful-inventions Willard had recently created. Little things, like ...

The Solar-Powered Toaster that exploded into a fireball. Not bad, if you liked your toast well done.

The Computer-Guided Eyebrow Plucker. Unfortunately, it didn't stop with the eyebrows—as the first hundred angry, bald customers proved.

The Turbo-Charged Pickle Jar Lid Opener. A great success, except for the twenty-seven kosher dills still embedded in Cody's kitchen ceiling.

"Hurry!" Willard called over his shoulder. "We must dispatch ourselves with expedience!"

"Do what with who?" Cody asked, looking up at his friend.

"We gotta go!"

●

The map light illuminated Mom's finger as she traced the winding road on the atlas. "Just one more mile," she murmured. Her voice was both hopeful and anxious.

"All right, sweetheart," Dad said as they shot through the thick woods. He tried to sound reassuring, but inside his fear continued to grow. *What if we don't get to the kids before they do?*

He glanced to his wife and thought back to the beginning.

●

Mom had been pregnant with their third child, Elijah. She had just left the florist's with a giant bouquet of daisies for her sister's birthday. As she walked—more like waddled—toward the car, a bearded old man with a tattered jacket stepped in front of her, bringing her to an abrupt stop.

He spoke quietly, almost in reverence. "Your son will work miracles."

She blinked, more than a little surprised. How had he known she was going to have a boy?

He continued. "The Scriptures speak of him."

"Who?" she asked, hoping to slip inside the car and get away from the crazy man—not an easy feat when one is holding a bouquet of flowers.

"Your son."

She stared at him a moment, then nodded slowly, uneasily, as she opened the car door and got inside. She locked the car and put the key in the ignition. She glanced back at the man, but when she turned he had vanished. The old man was nowhere to be seen.

Unfortunately, that was only the beginning of the strangeness. It soon got stranger.

Just after Elijah was born, Mom and Dad began to notice little things. Like how their baby laughed and cooed as if he saw something above his crib ... when there was nothing there at all.

Or the time he was in preschool and his teacher ran out of snacks ... or thought she did. No one could explain how, when she kept reaching into the graham cracker box, she never ran out of graham crackers—not until the last child was served. Amazing. Well, to everyone but Mom and Dad.

That was the good weird. But there was also the bad ...

More and more, they got the sense that people were watching them. Sometimes it was a dark blue car that followed them at a distance when they pushed the baby stroller down the street. Other times it was a tall, skinny man in overalls who always seemed to be trimming hedges or sweeping a sidewalk when they went outside.

Then came the fateful Saturday morning when the strange old man appeared once again—but this time on their doorstep.

Spotting him through the window, Mom called upstairs to Dad. "Mike! That man from the florist—it's him! He's here!"

Dad bounded down the stairs and threw open the door to confront him. But the old man said only three words:

"You must leave."

"Guess again," Dad said. "I don't know who you are or what's going on, but you're the one who has to leave."

The man shook his head. "No. You must go. For the boy's safety—and your own."

Dad snorted in disgust and started to shut the door when the old man raised his voice. "Please ... there is an organization."

Dad hesitated.

The old man continued. "They are watching your son to see if he is the one of whom the Scriptures speak. Once they are sure, they will move in."

Dad frowned. "Organization?"

"They are empowered by a dark and sinister force, and they will show no mercy when they come for him."

Dad bristled. "That's enough. If you don't leave right now, I'm calling the police. Do you understand?"

The old man remained. "You've seen his gifts."

"I don't know what you're talking about."

"You've seen his powers. You've seen—"

Without a word Dad slammed the door.

"I'm not sure if you should have done that," Mom said.

"The guy's a loony!" Dad replied angrily. He turned, checking through the door's peephole.

Nobody was there.

That was when they decided to pack up the kids and move ... the first time.

But no matter how they tried to hide Elijah's special gifts, the little guy would do something that caused people to start talking ... and asking questions.

Then, just a few days ago, a red-headed woman and two men with guns showed up at the house. Mom and Dad tried to act as decoys to draw them away, giving their children a chance to escape to safety, but the plan backfired. Instead, the parents were kidnapped and taken to a mysterious compound where they first encountered ... Shadow Man.

They had escaped. It was a miracle from God — there was no doubt about that.

But Shadow Man wasn't about to give up — there was no doubt about that either.

Chapter Three

Arrest

"We're going to *fly?!*" Cody's voice cracked. It hadn't done that since he was thirteen, but raw fear can do that to a guy. "*AGAIN?*"

"No," Willard chuckled, "we're not going to fly."

"Whew, that's good."

"Technically, we will simply be resisting gravity."

Somehow, that didn't make Cody feel much better.

"We must locate Piper's parents," Willard said as he slipped into his antigravity tennis shoes. "We must inform them of the tracking device my equipment has discovered under their car. This is the only way to warn them."

"If we survive," Cody said, giving the shoes a doubtful look.

Willard ignored him. "I've triangulated their last email transmission with their cell phone call. But we must proceed there quickly before we lose them."

Cody was silent, frowning down at the tops of his tennis shoes.

"Look, I know what you're thinking," Willard said. "You're recalling the time my Remote-Controlled Pencil Sharpener flew out the window, crashed into the power station, and shorted out the entire town for a week."

"Actually," Cody said, "I forgot that one."

"Then perhaps it was my Inviso-Bug Spray which I brought to summer camp that made us both invisible."

"Actually," Cody corrected, "it just made our clothes invisible."

"Ah, yes." Willard nodded. "That was rather embarrassing. However, I promise you there will be no such occurrences on this occasion."

"Don't you think we should at least test them?" Cody asked.

"Under normal circumstances, yes, you would be correct. A positive outcome of a trial run is crucial before the operation of any new device."

"Good!"

"However, we have no time."

"Bad!"

"I assure you, all my data indicates these shoes will perform perfectly."

Cody gave him a look. He knew Willard wanted to help. He also knew that not a single invention of his had ever worked ... well, had ever worked the way he'd planned for it to work. Still, Willard was right. The family was in trouble, and they had no time to waste. So, with a heavy sigh (and a prayer that someone somewhere would someday find their bodies) Cody slipped into the shoes and laced them up tightly.

Willard reached for the control panel strapped to his wrist and hit a flashing red button. "Hopefully, we won't have any problems. Hold on."

"What do you mean, *hopefully*?" Cody's voice cracked again. "And what do you mean, *hold on*?"

"I mean...

"WHOOOAAAAAAAH!"

Suddenly Willard shot up and hovered in the air. For that matter, so did...

"WHOOOAAAAAAAH!"

... Cody.

There was only one minor problem.

"We're upside down!" Cody shouted, dangling from his feet. He kicked and spun around in the air as he tried to right himself.

"Yes, I am aware of that fact, however ..."

"However what?"

"We have no time for repairs! We must depart now!"

Before Cody could protest, Willard pushed a little joystick on his control panel, and they took off. Still upside down. And still shouting.

"WHOOOAAAAAAAH!!"

●

Mom and Dad pulled to a stop at the agreed-upon location: the parking lot of the Desert Sands Motor Lodge. They sat quietly in the Jeep, holding each other's hand, waiting eagerly and impatiently for their children. Dad tried to relax, nervously drumming his free fingers on the dash while Mom peered anxiously into the night.

"Mike!" she suddenly shouted.

He sat up and looked through the window, just in time to spot a pair of headlights coming up the highway. They belonged to the RV.

"It's them!"

●

Piper, peering out the window of the RV, gave a start. Her heart leapt as she cried out. "There they are!"

"I see them!" Zach exclaimed. He pressed down on the accelerator, urging the old vehicle forward.

Piper spun around and, in her excitement, gave Elijah a hug. The family would be together again at last. Maybe now things would finally get back to normal. No more kidnappings. No more escapes. Soon they'd be back home in the family room, munching popcorn, and watching the latest DVD.

The motor home pulled up beside the Jeep, and the doors to both vehicles flew open. Zach, Piper, and Elijah spilled out of the RV, while Mom and Dad raced out of the Jeep. Before they knew it, everyone was wrapped in one giant bear hug.

"Okay, okay," Zach gasped. "I can't breathe, give me some air."

Piper was enduring her own brand of suffocating, but the love felt too good to complain.

Finally they broke up, Mom wiping her eyes with the sleeve of her jacket. "Are you kids all okay?"

"We're fine," Piper said, blinking back her own tears. "What about you guys?"

"Couldn't be better," Mom laughed and threw her arms around them again for more hugs and suffocation.

"Whew," Dad waved his hand in front of his nose. "Son, what's that smell?"

Piper rolled her eyes. "Nuclear Burrito breath."

Elijah giggled as the family joked and hugged and teased. After all this time, they were together. How long they stood in the parking lot like that, nobody knows. But eventually, they split apart and headed back to the vehicles. Mom and the kids would ride in the Jeep, while Dad would follow behind in the RV.

It was time to go home.

●

Zach slid into the front seat beside Mom as she started up the Jeep and pulled onto the road. Elijah sat with Piper in the back. He snuggled against her and quickly fell asleep.

"I've got a ton of questions," Zach said.

"Me too," Piper added.

"Me three," Mom exclaimed.

"Okay," Zach said. "It was kinda weird when we came home from school and there's the vacuum cleaner in the middle of the floor—"

"Along with all the clothes from the dryer," Piper added, "and the dirty dishes piled up in the sink."

"Yeah," Zach said, "it was like you guys got raptured or something."

Mom nodded. "Okay, let me tell you what happened. I was watching the news on television when—" Her eyes caught something in the rearview mirror.

"What's wrong?" Zach asked.

Piper turned and saw Dad flashing his high beams at them. "Mom?"

"I see," Mom said. She had also seen the bright blue lights of a police car flashing behind Dad.

"Oh, no," she groaned.

"What?" Zach asked.

"Your father is getting pulled over."

Chapter Four

The Trap

Back in the RV, Dad had spotted the police car and signaled Mom. He pulled onto the gravel shoulder and was relieved to see his wife doing the same up ahead.

He watched in his mirror as the police officer approached, the blue light on top of his car still flashing. The officer's flashlight beam poked around inside the RV until it finally arrived at Dad's side. He tapped on the glass and motioned Dad to roll down his window.

"May I see your license please?"

"Certainly," Dad said as he reached into his back pocket and pulled out his wallet. He opened it, produced his license and handed it to the officer.

The man took it, shined his flashlight on the picture, and then on Dad.

Squinting in the bright light, Dad asked, "Is there a problem, Officer?"

Without answering the question, the man ordered gruffly, "Step out of the vehicle, sir."

Dad opened the door and obeyed. "Is this really necessary? I don't think I was speeding. Maybe if you just told me—"

The officer cut him off. "Come around to the rear of the vehicle."

Again, Dad did as he was told.

"Put your hands behind your back."

"Officer, what's going on?"

"Put your hands behind your back, and I'll explain."

Dad shrugged and obeyed. That's when he felt and heard the metallic *click* of handcuffs.

"You're under arrest."

"What?!"

The officer said nothing but looked ahead to the Jeep where his partner was also ordering Mom and the children outside.

•

Piper could tell her mother was confused and more than a little angry. "I don't understand," she was saying to the officer. "What do you mean, we're under arrest?"

"Please remain quiet. We'll explain later. Put your hands behind your back."

"Mom," Piper said, "what's going—"

"Please, put your hands behind your back."

"Mom?"

Reluctantly, Mom obeyed. Immediately her hands were cuffed.

Elijah tugged on Piper's shirt, and she glanced down to see his worried expression. "It's going to be all right," she said.

But the look in his eyes said he knew better.

Zach knew better too. "You're no cop!" he said.

"Put your hands behind your back and keep quiet."

"You cannot arrest my children! We have done nothing wrong!" Mom cried out in protest, straining against the handcuffs.

"Real cops don't act like this," Zach insisted. "And real cops don't drive Hummers."

Piper whirled back around to the police car and squinted. He was right. It *wasn't* a police car! It was hard to see, with the RV lights between them, but in the darkness she could just make out the shape of a Humvee.

"It's a trick!" Piper yelled. "Mom, it's a trap!"

Before anyone could respond, Elijah suddenly took off running.

"Hey!" The officer lunged for him, but the little guy was too quick. He dodged the man and ran toward Dad and the RV.

In the confusion, Zach broke free and raced into the darkness of the woods.

"You! Stop! Get back here!"

Piper tried to follow but she only managed a step or two before the officer spun around and grabbed her from behind.

"Let go of me!" she yelled.

"You're staying right—"

"Let go of me!

He produced another pair of handcuffs and before she knew what was happening he was cuffing her, too. "You're staying here!" he ordered. Then he spun around and took off after Elijah.

"Run, Eli!" Piper shouted. "Run!"

She could tell the RV's lights blinded her little brother as he held up his hands, shielding his eyes from their brightness. Only then did she see the shadowy form standing in front of those lights.

"Elijah, look out!"

But she was too late. He ran straight into the folds of a large black cloak that quickly wrapped itself around his tiny body.

Mom saw it too and gasped:

"Shadow Man!"

●

Elijah sat in the back of the speeding Hummer trying not to cry. Beside him was the dark, mysterious man of shadows. Up ahead, one so-called officer was driving the RV. The other was driving the Jeep.

And far behind them, handcuffed and left alongside the road were Mom, Dad, and Piper.

The man of shadows pressed the intercom button and spoke to the driver. "There isss a river on the other ssside of thisss tunnel," he hissed. "Tell the driversss to leave the other cars where they are and join usss."

"Yes sir," the driver answered and reached for his two-way radio.

Out the window Elijah caught a glimpse of someone standing next to the road. Someone who looked just like the old man who had explained the Bible verses to him back at the restaurant ... and exactly like the homeless man who had helped them escape back in Los Angeles.

The little guy closed his eyes and silently began to pray.

Suddenly, the driver slammed on his brakes and they skidded, barely missing the Jeep and RV which were stopped just ahead.

"What isss thisss?" Shadow Man growled.

Elijah opened his eyes and saw that the road ahead had been blocked by a van—the same dark green van that had been following them ever since Los Angeles. A moment later, the woman with flaming red hair and her two assistants tumbled out and raced toward the RV.

Angrily, Shadow Man opened his own door and stepped out, "What are you doing?"

In the confusion, Elijah hoped to escape. He reached for the door and opened it gently. But immediately an alarm began to beep.

"Hey!" the driver looked in the mirror. "What are you—"

Elijah hopped out and was about to make a run for it, but the driver was too quick. He leaped from the car and grabbed the boy. Elijah put up a fight, squirming and twisting, but it did no good. Within seconds the driver had tossed him back into the car and slammed the door.

As the driver slipped back behind the wheel, Elijah reached for the door handle, hoping to try again. But the driver spotted him and hit the auto lock. It came down with a soft *click.*

He grinned sinisterly at Elijah through the mirror. The boy slumped into the seat, unsure what to do. He watched as the driver spoke into his two-way radio.

"What's happening up there?" the man asked.

A gruff voice answered. "It's Monica and her two goons!"

"Oh no," the driver groaned.

"She didn't know we got the kid. Thought she'd try to nab him from the RV."

The driver shook his head. "Idiots."

Elijah looked back out his window and was happy to

again see the old man. He stood at the edge of the woods and gave the slightest nod to the boy. Immediately, the lock to the door clicked up.

The driver was too busy talking into the radio to notice. "What's Shadow Man gonna do to her?" he asked.

Elijah reached for the door handle.

"I dunno," the gruff voice replied. "But I sure wouldn't want to be in her shoes."

In one quick move, Elijah yanked open the door and leaped out.

"Hey!" the driver shouted. But he was too late. Elijah was already dashing into the dark forest.

Chapter Five

On the Run

Piper wanted to be strong. She stood on the side of the road, trying to stop the tears from coming, but she couldn't. And with her hands cuffed behind her back, she couldn't wipe them away either.

How could things get any worse? Not only was she handcuffed, but so were Mom and Dad. Plus her little brother had been kidnapped, and Zach was missing. Plus they were on a road so remote she doubted that they'd see any cars for the next hour ... or day ... or year.

"Maybe we should figure out where the nearest town is," Dad suggested, "and start walking to it."

"What if Zach tries to come back here?" Mom asked.

Dad sighed. She was right, of course, but he found it almost impossible to wait around when his youngest child was in such great danger.

"Are you okay, sweetheart?"

Piper looked over to see her mother watching her. "Yeah," she sniffed, then glanced away. "I'm fine." But she knew she wasn't. And she knew Mom knew.

"We can't let ourselves get discouraged." Piper could hear the thickness in her mother's voice. She knew she was talking as much to herself as to her. "We're going to be all right. God's looking out for us."

Piper blew the hair out of her eyes and breathed out slowly in a long, quiet sigh. If this was God's version of looking out for them, she'd hate to see what would happen if he didn't. It wasn't that she doubted God. She knew he existed and all. But if he was supposed to be so loving, why had he let all this hard stuff happen to them? Why didn't he just—

"Shhh," Dad motioned them to get down. "There's something in the woods."

Piper turned to look behind them. It was true, something was moving in the bushes!

Dad eased himself protectively in front of Mom and Piper. Not that he could do much with his hands cuffed behind his back.

The rustling came closer.

"What is it?" Mom whispered. "A bear?"

Dad motioned them to crouch closer to the ground. They did so, still peering into the darkness.

It was fifteen feet away.

"Should we run?" Piper whispered.

Dad shook his head.

It continued approaching until it was ten feet from them.

Now Piper could make out a shape in the shadows. It was big and dark—

Eight more feet.

Almost the size of a man.

Piper watched, refusing to look away. If she was going to die, she wanted to know how. She wanted to see it coming and face it down.

Seven feet.

It was nearly on top of them. For the briefest second she caught a glimpse of what might be a face.

Six feet.

Suddenly, it opened what must have been its mouth and let out the world's biggest. . .

BELCH!

This was immediately followed by a terrible stench. A stench that could only come from a. . .

"Nuclear Burrito!" Piper cried.

"Hey, everybody!" Zach grinned.

Dad could only shake his head. "Zachary . . ."

Before he could continue, Zach stepped aside. "Look what I found!" And there, behind him, stood little Elijah, smiling his biggest smile.

●

The family walked the twisting mountain road for nearly half an hour before they stumbled upon their vehicles. Above them, up on the hillside, Shadow Man's thugs were searching the forest, the beams of their flashlights crisscrossing back and forth.

"What's going on?" Zach whispered.

"They're searching for Eli," Dad answered.

"What do we do?"

Dad motioned them back behind some boulders. Once there, they worked out a plan. Piper listened, trying to concentrate, but it was hard to pay attention with the handcuffs cutting deeper and deeper into her wrists.

Finally, the plan was set.

Since Zach had no handcuffs, he went first. He dashed across the road to the Jeep, keeping as low as possible. Once he arrived, he quietly opened the back door. Leaving it open, he crossed around to the driver's side, opened that door, and slid in behind the wheel where he ducked out of sight.

Now it was Elijah's turn.

He ran across the road and dove through the back door Zach had left open.

Next came Piper. It was hard for her to climb into the car with the handcuffs holding her arms behind her back. Zach and Elijah pulled, and she twisted and squirmed until she finally made it inside.

Then it was Mom's turn.

And finally Dad, who took some extra pulling.

Once everyone was inside, Elijah quietly pulled the door shut.

"Okay, Zach," Dad whispered. "Go for it!"

Zach turned on the ignition, and the Jeep roared to life.

In the woods, the flashlights stopped moving. They all turned and merged into one giant beam ... pointed at the Jeep.

Zach hit the gas. The tires spun, spitting gravel, and the family took off.

Piper looked over her shoulder to see the flashlights bouncing to the cars. It would take a couple minutes before they arrived and started after the family, but she knew they would soon be coming.

Zach pressed the accelerator, picking up speed.

"Be careful, Son," Dad warned. "These curves are sharp."

Zach nodded and slowed slightly. For a moment silence filled the car. But Piper had too many questions for it to last long.

"Um, Dad?"

"Yes."

"Now's probably not a good time to ask, but . . ."

"Go ahead," he said. "Ask away."

"Okay. I'm wondering, I mean, if it's not too much bother, could you tell us, you know—*what's going on?*" She didn't mean to yell, it just sort of came out that way.

Mom and Dad traded looks. Dad arched an eyebrow. Mom hesitated, and then gave a little nod. Dad returned it and began.

"We can't tell you everything, because those thugs want the same information. The less you know, the safer you'll all be. But we can tell you this much." He took a breath. "Your brother is . . . well, he's special."

"Thanks!" Zach called from behind the wheel.

"Not you," Piper said.

"You're special too," Dad chuckled, and then he grew serious. "It's just, well, there's a lot more to Elijah than you realize."

Piper looked over to her little brother who was curled up in Mom's lap, his eyes already closed. It wasn't a big surprise. Lots of times when everybody was nervous, he was completely relaxed. Other times when everyone was relaxed, he was really nervous.

Mom looked at Elijah and continued the explanation. "We knew something was up, even when he was a baby."

"Like what?" Zach asked.

"Oh, just little things."

"Such as?"

Once again Mom traded looks with Dad.

"I don't think you're ready for that information," Dad said. "Not just yet."

Zach grunted his disapproval from the driver's seat.

"We'll tell you when it's time," Mom said. "But for now, the important thing to know is that Elijah is special. And that there are others—an organization of others—who also know it."

"That's why they want him? Because he's special?" Zach asked.

"Yes."

"But there's something else."

Piper turned to Dad, waiting for more.

He hesitated just a moment before continuing. "We're in a battle. We've been in one for a while, but now it's getting worse."

Zach motioned over his shoulder. "You mean with those goons back there."

Dad shook his head. "It's more than that. It's a spiritual battle."

"Like the devil and stuff?" Piper asked.

Dad nodded. "Yes."

She felt goose bumps rise and crawl across her arms as a shiver went through her body.

Zach had a different response. "Cool!"

Piper cleared her throat. "That sounds kind of, you know . . . scary."

Dad shook his head. "It doesn't have to be. Remember, as Christians, we have power over the enemy."

Piper did remember, but it didn't make her any more relaxed.

"That's the war we're fighting," Dad said. "And that's the war we're going to win."

Piper looked from her mother to her father. She was

grateful for their faith. And she had little doubt that they had enough to succeed.

She just wasn't sure she did.

She looked out the window in time to see a jagged fork of lightning cut through the darkness. A moment later, the thunder followed, pounding and rolling through the sky.

●

Meanwhile, in the Hummer, Shadow Man was in no hurry to catch up with the family. The tracker attached to the bottom of the Jeep would always tell him where they were. No matter what they tried or what they did, the family would never be able to get away.

Never.

Chapter Six

The Crash

Zach glanced into the rearview mirror. He knew the bad guys weren't far behind. Up above, the sky flashed with bright, jagged forks of lightning. Thunder rumbled as Dad continued his discussion on spiritual warfare.

"Remember when you were all kids?" Dad said. "How I made you memorize Ephesians 6 from the Bible?"

"How could we forget," Zach groaned. "You had us say it like a billion times."

"Do you still remember it?" Dad asked.

Piper spoke up from the back: *"For our struggle is not against flesh and blood, but against the rulers ..."*

Reluctantly, Zach join in, *"... against the authorities, against the powers of this dark world and against the spiritual forces of evil in the heavenly realms."*

Dad nodded. "And the next verse?"

Zach frowned, but Piper continued:

"Therefore put on the full armor of God, so that when the day of evil comes, you may be able to stand your ground."

"Very good," Dad smiled. "I guess you were listening after all."

Mom spoke up. "And do you remember the weapons God gives us to fight with?"

"That one's easy," Zach said. *"The sword of the spirit, which is the word of God."*

"And the shield of faith," Piper added.

"And prayer," Zach added. "It's not on the list, but we've seen it do some major damage." He glanced in the mirror and spotted his sister.

"And don't forget worship," Piper said. "Like singing to God and stuff."

Mom agreed. "The devil really hates that. Remember how we used to sing, Jesus loves me, this I know?" As the family nodded, all remembering, the radio suddenly crackled to life.

"Come in, Dawkins family. Dawkins family, can you hear me?"

Everyone froze ... until Zach broke out laughing.

"What is that?" Mom asked.

"Not *what*," Zach grinned. "*Who*. It's Willard, good ol' Willard."

"On our radio?" Piper asked.

Dad motioned out the window. "Look at that!"

Two shapes were flying about a dozen feet above the car and to the right.

"It's Willard and Cody!" Zach exclaimed. At least he thought it was. It was kinda hard to tell with them hanging upside down and all. It was even harder to tell when Willard zigged and zagged, just missing a billboard.

Unfortunately, Cody wasn't quite so lucky. He zagged when he should have zigged and busted through the billboard.

"Oh, no!" Piper pressed against her window and watched the aerial acrobatics.

Now they were bouncing up and down like jet-propelled pogo sticks.

This time it was Cody's voice they heard over the radio. But he didn't do much talking. In fact, it was just one word. Still, you could definitely tell he wasn't thrilled about what was happening:

"WIL-IL-IL-IL-IL-IL-LARD-ARD-ARD-ARD-ARD ..."

A moment later and Willard's voice came back on the radio: *"Dawkins family, listen up. There is a transmitting device planted on your Jeep. You are being tracked and must—"*

Lightning lit up the sky around them, and static filled the radio.

"Are they all right?" Mom gasped.

Dad leaned forward to look up through the windshield and search the sky.

So did Zach, which explains why he didn't see the sharp bend in the road just before the bridge.

"Look out!" Dad shouted.

But he was too late. The Jeep shot off the side of the road, and suddenly they were airborne. Mom and Piper screamed as the car sailed through the air, heading straight for the river.

"Hang on!" Dad yelled.

The nose of the car dropped, and Zach braced himself as the river raced toward them.

"Everybody hang—"

They slammed into the water. Zach's seat belt dug into his chest as airbags exploded all around. The Jeep righted itself and floated as icy cold water poured in through the floorboards. Everyone was shouting and screaming.

Zach tried to open his door but couldn't. His mind raced, remembering something he'd heard—how if a car goes under water, the outside pressure keeps the doors shut.

"Roll down your windows!" he yelled.

"That's crazy!" Piper shouted. "We don't want to let in more water!

"He's right!" Dad shouted. "Do it!"

Elijah obeyed. He reached past Piper and cranked down the window as fast as he could. That's when the horror hit Zach. His mother, father, and sister were all handcuffed! They'd never be able to swim out! He'd have to save them all.

The river rose to their laps and continued filling the car.

Zach reached into the water, found the seat belt and unbuckled himself. He bent and squirmed until his head and shoulders were out the window, then he pulled himself the rest of the way.

"Zach!" Dad shouted. He turned to see his father struggling to open his own window. "Grab Piper!"

Zach nodded, panting heavily, and swam back to Piper's side. The water was up to her chest now. She'd managed to get her head through the window and was pushing against the seat with her legs, but with her hands cuffed behind her back, she could go no further.

"Zach, help me!" she cried, her eyes full of panic.

He grabbed her shoulders and pulled. She yelped as her stomach scraped across the window until she was finally out. But there was still no way to swim with her hands cuffed.

He wrapped his arm around her waist. Together they kicked and swam against the icy current. More than once they went under, but they kept fighting back up, choking and coughing until, at last, Zach's feet hit the river bottom. Then Piper's. They sloshed and stumbled toward the bank until they arrived and collapsed onto the muddy shore.

But where were the others?

Zach spun around to look. The Jeep had sunk almost to its roof. Without thinking, he dove back into the river and swam toward it.

Gasping for air, he finally arrived. Elijah was helping Mom out. Dad had managed to open his window, but he was too big to make it through the opening and the door was jammed!

Zach took a gulp of air and dove under water to reenter the Jeep through his side. His father's face was up against the ceiling, gulping breaths from the shrinking pocket of air. Zach tucked in his legs and spun around until his feet landed against Dad's door. He kicked it once, twice, three times before it finally gave way and opened.

With lungs burning for air, he pushed out through his window and resurfaced, taking in deep, gulping breaths. He turned and spotted Dad outside the car frantically kicking his feet to stay above the water.

"HANG ON!" he shouted. He swam around the car and grabbed the back of Dad's shirt. Together, they kicked and swam toward shore, where they finally arrived, exhausted.

"Elijah!" Mom cried.

They turned to see Mom had also arrived—obviously with the help of Elijah. But the little guy was nowhere to be found.

"The current!" she cried. "It carried him away!" She staggered to her feet, searching. "He was here and then ... Elijah!"

Zach rose to his knees, also looking, also shouting. "ELIJAH! ELIJAH!"

And then he spotted him. On the *other* side. The outline of a man was reaching down and pulling him out of the water.

Joy filled Zach. They'd made it! Despite the crash, despite everyone nearly losing their life, they were all safe and sound!

Well, not quite.

Because Dad had also spotted Elijah. And instead of shouting or cheering, he gasped a single word—a name that chilled Zach even more than the icy water.

"Shadow Man ..."

Chapter Seven

Going Down

Mom, Dad, Zach, and Piper stood on the beach, dripping and panting, staring in disbelief at the far shore.

Should they try to find a town and tell the police? Or should they head back to Shadow Man's headquarters and rescue Elijah?

Not that it made any difference. They were so lost they didn't know which direction to go anyway ... until they heard a very familiar voice screaming overhead:

"WATCH OUT!"

Actually, two very familiar voices ...

"YOU WATCH OUT!"

"I THOUGHT YOU KNEW HOW TO STEER THESE THINGS!"

Piper peered up into the night just in time to see two bodies . . .

"AAAAAUGH!"

"WHOAAAAA!"

. . . drop from the sky and . . .

Ker-*SPLASH!*

Ker-*SPLUNK!*

. . . fall into the river in front of them.

Willard and Cody surfaced, coughing and sputtering as they made their way toward the riverbank.

"Don't worry, he says," Cody was shaking his head. "*Trust me*, he says, *I'll find them*, he says."

"Well I did, didn't I?" Willard argued.

"And nearly got us killed!"

"Honestly," Willard pushed the dripping hair out of his eyes, "sometimes you can be so picky."

Piper smiled in spite of herself. Even though everything had gone wrong, it was good to see them. Especially Cody. It wasn't that she liked him or anything. She just liked being around him . . . even if his presence did make her a thousand times more klutzy.

"Are you two all right?" Dad asked.

"Couldn't be better," Willard answered. "Just great."

To which Cody, digging water out of his ear, replied, "This is obviously a new definition of *great*." He spotted Piper and gave her a little nod. She nodded back, suddenly finding it difficult to breathe.

Zach motioned to the sky. "Did you see any towns from up there?"

Willard shook his head. "Not for at least fifty miles."

"Well," Dad sighed. "I guess that rules out the police."

"What about a fortress?" Mom asked. "Big and long, made out of rock—almost like a castle."

"Yeah," Cody said, "we saw that."

Willard agreed. "I estimate some twenty miles back down that winding road."

"Or," Cody motioned behind them, "a couple miles straight through those woods."

Piper and her family traded looks. They had their answer.

"What about those handcuffs?" Willard said.

"Any suggestions?" Dad asked.

Willard dug into his pants. "Perhaps this combination picklock/bottle opener I always carry will be of some assistance."

Again Piper and her family traded looks. Willard could be a pain, but sometimes, like now, the pain was definitely worth it.

●

Ninety long minutes later they were crouched down in the woods, just outside Shadow Man's headquarters.

"There's nobody here," Zach said.

And he was right. As far as Piper could tell there were no lights, no movement, no nothing. She blew the hair out of her eyes in frustration. They'd just waded through dark and spooky woods with only Willard's and Cody's flashlights. They just risked being eaten by bears or who knew what, received a gazillion mosquito bites, and been scratched by every branch and rock in their path only to discover that nobody was home.

"I wouldn't bet on that," Dad said. "It's a big place. Maybe they've got him hidden somewhere."

"So are we going in to find him?" Zach asked.

Dad hesitated a moment, then nodded. "You and I will sneak in." He turned to the others. "The rest of you stay here where it's safe. If we find anybody, we'll—"

Mom interrupted, "No, I don't think so."

He came to a stop. "What's that?"

Mom thrust out her chin the way she always did when she got stubborn. "If you're going in, I'm going with you."

"Judy," Dad said, "you know how dangerous it is. You know what Shadow Man can—"

"He's my baby!" she blurted out. Then, recovering, she took a breath and repeated, "If you're going in, I'm going in. I'm not staying here without you—not when my Elijah is in there."

"Me too," Piper said as she stepped forward.

"And you may count us in," Willard added.

Dad shook his head. "No. Absolutely not. It's too—"

"Dad ..." Piper interrupted, "he's my brother."

"And our friend," Cody added. "We didn't come all this way just to stand around and be afraid."

For a long moment, Dad stood looking at the group. It was obvious he was outnumbered and no one would change their mind. He heaved a heavy sigh, "All right, then."

Piper's heart pounded. She was excited and terrified at the same time.

"Where do we start?" Zach asked.

"Your mother and I escaped from that door over there." Dad pointed to the far end of the building. "With any luck it's still unlocked."

"What about surveillance cameras?" Willard asked.

"That's a chance we'll have to take. Just stay low . . . and hope for the best."

Everybody nodded.

"All right, then," Dad said. "I'll go first. If the coast is clear I'll signal you. Any questions?"

There were none.

"Okay, then." He crouched low, took a breath, and started off.

Once he arrived, he pressed flat against the wall and pushed open the door to look inside. A moment later he turned back to the group and motioned them to follow.

Zach took off, followed by Mom, Cody, and Willard. Piper brought up the rear—not because she was scared, but because it was hard to run crouched over, especially when she was busy praying for her life.

Dad held the door as they entered. It was a cold, stone hallway, much like a castle. Up ahead, the hallway split into a *T*, and a dozen yards beyond that it split again.

"We'll break up into groups of two," Dad whispered. "Check every room. And be careful!"

They agreed and, for the briefest second, Piper wasn't sure who to go with until . . .

"Hey, Piper."

She turned to see Cody.

"You're with me, okay?"

If her heart was pounding before, it was doing cartwheels now. Not only cartwheels, but jumping jacks, back flips, and . . . well, you get the picture. Fortunately she was able to swallow back most of the emotion and come up with a squeaky little, "Sure."

Cody grabbed her hand and they took the hallway to the left. Ten feet ahead was the first door. When they arrived, Cody tested the knob. He turned it and pushed it open.

Looking inside, Piper shivered. It was dark and completely empty, except for the squeaking of mice scurrying out of sight.

Cody turned on his flashlight and took a step inside. "I wonder what this place used to be."

Piper followed, inching her way into the room. To the right of the doorway, she noticed a switch. But instead of a normal up and down switch, this one was round. Curious, she gave it a little twist.

"AUGH!" Cody yelled as the floor tilted.

Piper leaped back into the hallway, but the floor tipped so quickly that Cody, who was further inside, didn't have a chance. He lost his balance and fell, clawing at the wood floor as he slipped toward the far wall and the darkness appearing below it.

"Cody!"

The floor continued tilting, growing steeper and steeper.

"Hang on!" she cried. She dropped to her hands and knees. Careful to stay in the hallway, she reached as far as she could into the room. "Take my hand!"

He reached out, but they just missed.

Piper stretched further, clinging to the door post with one hand as she leaned into the tilting room.

Cody dug in, half-scrambling, half-leaping, until their hands touched. Piper grabbed hold and held on tightly as he pulled himself up the floor and finally into the hallway where he collapsed.

"Are you okay?" she gasped.

"Yeah," he said, trying to catch his breath. "Thanks."

"Look!" she pointed.

By now the floor was completely vertical, straight up and down ... and still it turned.

They watched in amazement as the flipside of the floor appeared ... complete with a stainless steel desk, black leather chair, and a six-foot floor lamp. In front of it rested a black leather sofa. Piper guessed the furniture had been screwed into the floor to keep it from falling when it was upside down. But, strangest of all, in the center of the room, was a weird glass chamber shaped like the bud of a flower—big enough for somebody to stand inside.

Dad called out from down the hall, "Are you guys all right?"

Piper turned to see Mom and Dad running to them. Zach and Willard were right behind. They'd obviously heard her cries.

"Yeah," she said, "we're okay."

Suddenly Mom came to a stop and gasped. Dad reached out to steady her.

"What?" Piper asked.

"It's where we were interrogated," Dad said. He stepped around the kids and with a breath for courage, entered the room. "It's Shadow Man's office."

Never one to be afraid (or think before he leapt) Zach followed Dad inside. He spotted the round switch and reached for it. "Hm, I wonder what this—"

"Zach!" Piper shouted.

But she was too late. He turned it, and once again the floor tilted ... the other way!

Now it was Dad's turn to shout, "AUGH!"

"Turn it back!" Piper yelled, "Turn the switch the other way!"

But Zach was too busy leaping out of the room to hear.

Piper reached past him. Keeping her feet in the hall, she stretched around the wall to the switch and cranked it hard in the opposite direction.

A good idea ... except she turned it too far and the floor reversed direction ... throwing Dad in the air like a pancake.

"AAAUGH!!"

The floor kept turning, and by the time he landed, it was so steep he slid into the desk.

"AAAAAUUGHH!"

He clutched the desk legs for all he was worth as the floor finished flipping, and he completely disappeared.

"Dad!" Zach yelled.

"What happened?!" Mom cried. "What did you do with your father?!"

Piper fumbled with the switch, turning it back the opposite direction until, once again, the floor flipped to reveal the high-tech office ... and Dad, hanging onto the desk.

He looked over to Piper as he tried catching his breath. He did his best not to yell, but she could tell he was pretty upset: "DON'T YOU EVER ... (*pant, pant*) ... TOUCH THAT ... (*gasp, gasp*) ... SWITCH AGAIN!"

Piper nodded hard, making it clear she understood.

"Quite fascinating," Willard said. He stuck his head inside the office and spotted another button on the opposite side of the door. "However, I wonder what this one—"

"Don't!" Piper cried. But she was too late.

"—does."

Dad braced himself for another ride, but absolutely nothing happened ... well, except for the panel on the wall behind the desk suddenly sliding open.

"Cool," Zach said as he reentered the room and strolled toward it. "I wonder where it goes."

Dad rose to his feet and joined him.

"Be careful, you two," Mom called.

They moved closer.

With rising curiosity, Willard and Cody took a tentative step into the office. So did Piper.

"What do you see?" Mom called to Dad.

"It looks like some sort of elevator." Dad stepped into it.

Zach joined him.

"An elevator?" Mom asked. Against her better judgment, she also stepped into the office.

"Hey," Zach said, reaching for a switch inside the elevator. "Here's another one of those round—

"DON'T—"

"—knobs." He gave it a twist. Once again the floor tilted toward the elevator, giving everyone a chance to...

"AUUGHHH!"

... as they tumbled, bounced, and rolled their way toward the open elevator.

One after another they landed inside...

"Ooof!"

"Oaaf!"

"Your elbow's in my ear!"

"Sorry!"

... until they were one giant mound of people. And before they could untangle themselves, the panel door *swiiished* shut and the elevator dropped.

Chapter Eight

The Cave

Piper thought the screaming and falling would never end. But finally, the elevator stopped, and the panel door slid open to reveal a cold, dark cave. It might have been a relief, except she hated cold, dark caves even worse than out-of-control, falling elevators.

Dad was the first to step out. When he was sure it was safe, he motioned the others to follow.

One by one they filed out.

"Be sure to keep our buddy system," he said. "There're lots of tunnels branching off, and we don't want anyone getting lost down here."

Dad and Mom led the way, followed by Zach and Willard. Piper and Cody brought up the rear. As they made their way forward, Piper began to feel a strange uneasiness—almost as if someone or some*thing* was watching them.

And then she heard it. A scraping sound. Behind them.

Was it her imagination? It must have been.

They continued walking until—there it was again.

And again.

Almost like footsteps. And they were getting closer!

Mustering all of her courage, she stole a quick look over her shoulder. That's when she saw what looked like a flash of red fire and two black shadows coming toward them!

She screamed. Dad shouted something, but Piper didn't stick around to hear. Seized with panic, she began running. Not forward—there were too many people in the way. Instead, she darted into the first passageway she found and ran for her life.

She only looked over her shoulder once. But that was enough to miss seeing the giant hole in front of her. The giant hole that she tripped, stumbled, and fell into ... screaming all the way.

●

Mom wasn't sure how far she'd run when Dad pulled them into a small nook of one of the tunnels. Zach and Willard were nowhere to be seen. Neither were Piper or Cody. Everyone had taken off in different directions.

Well, almost everyone.

It seemed they were still being followed by the red fire and two dark figures, which soon became visible as the woman with fiery hair and her two goons.

"Nice work!" the redhead shrieked. "He sent us back to find them, and now they're gone!"

"Sorry, can we leave now?" the biggest one asked.

"You're nothing but an overgrown chicken!"

"Sorry, can we leave now?"

"I agree with Bruno," the skinny one said. "This place really creeps me out."

"So can we leave now?"

"Quiet!" the redhead bellowed.

As the yelling drew closer, Dad reached into his pocket.

"What are you doing?" Mom whispered.

"If we stay here, they're bound to find us."

"So ..."

"So I'll scare them off."

"With what?"

He proudly pulled out a pocket breath sprayer. "This!"

Mom blinked, wondering if there was a chance he'd lost his mind.

He explained. "When I give you the signal, shine that flashlight on me."

Now she was sure he'd lost his mind. "What?"

The shouting voices were almost there. Without further explanation, Dad wrapped his hand around the breath spray, stepped forward, and shouted, "Stop!" His voice echoed through the cave.

The woman and her goons stumbled to a stop.

Dad nodded to Mom who reluctantly turned on the flashlight. It cast a giant shadow of him against the wall. And, as he held the breath spray toward them with his index finger pointed out, it looked like a very big man holding a very big gun.

"Stay where you are!" he shouted in his deepest voice. "Don't make me use this!"

It must have done the trick. The goons leapt back, spun around, and ran away as fast as they could.

Mom could only stare.

When the coast was clear, Dad turned to her and smiled. "So what did you think?"

Mom shook her head. "Amazing."

"Thanks," he said then gave his mouth a good spritz of spearmint breath spray.

●

Piper woke up to a pounding headache. She wasn't sure how long she'd been unconscious, but the hard cave floor—complete with rocks jabbing into her back—told her she wasn't exactly dead ... at least not yet. Then there was the darkness. It made no difference if her eyes were open or closed—the blackness was complete, and she couldn't see anything around her.

Then she heard the sounds. Whisperings. Quiet, like the wind blowing through leaves.

A chill rippled across her shoulders.

The whisperings grew louder—eerie and haunting as they echoed against the cave walls.

She reached into the darkness for her flashlight. It had to be there, somewhere.

By now the whisperings were so close she could almost hear words.

She scrapped a rock with her knee, and the whispering stopped—just a few feet away.

Where was that flashlight?! Where had it dropped?

She could hear breathing now. Quiet, and very close.

At last she felt the flashlight. She grabbed it, making

sure it pointed the right direction. Her fingers searched for the on/off switch. There it was.

The breathing was practically on top of her.

She took a silent breath of her own. It was now or never. She let go a bloodcurdling scream while snapping on the blazing light.

Three pairs of boys' eyes widened like saucers. The pair with the glasses rolled up into their head and fell out of sight   as Willard hit the ground with a dull *THUD*.

Chapter Nine

Darkness Tightens Its Grip

"Willard!" Cody dropped to his knees and knelt over his friend. "Willard, wake up!" He reached down and slapped his face.

Willard's eyes popped open. "OW!" He immediately slapped Cody back.

Zach had left their side to check on Piper. "You okay?"

"Yeah," she said in a shaky voice. "Thanks for finding me. Where are Mom and Dad?"

"They're next on our list," Zach said as he helped her to her feet.

But she had barely stood before she felt it. "Whoa ... what's that?"

The guys exchanged glances.

"What's what?" Zach asked.

Piper frowned. "I don't know, it's like . . ." She wanted to say it was like a giant wave of selfishness had washed over her. That, suddenly, the only thing she cared about was what was best for her. But admitting that was far too embarrassing, especially in front of Cody.

So, instead of answering, she simply shrugged, "I'm not . . . sure."

Cody nervously cleared his throat. "Actually, we're all feeling things."

Willard added, "And the further we proceed into this cave, the stronger those emotions become."

Piper gave a shudder. The selfish part of her wanted to run away, to let the others find her parents, to let them save her little brother. She had her own life to live. Why should she care? But she fought against the feelings, refusing to give in.

"So, which way?" Cody asked.

"That's an ignorant question," Willard snapped. "We press on, of course."

The rudeness surprised Piper. That wasn't like Willard at all.

He continued. "We are already aware of what is behind us. We are unaware of what lies ahead." Without waiting for the others to agree, he started forward.

"I'm—I'm not sure that's such a good idea," Cody said. His voice sounded unsure, almost like he was afraid.

"Why not?" Willard demanded.

"Because," Cody glanced from side to side. "Because we . . ."

Willard rolled his eyes. "Out with it, we don't have the entire day."

Piper came to his rescue. "Because we should pray first."

Now it was Zach's turn to show contempt. "Oh, brother."

Piper turned to him in surprise. Zach had never felt that way about prayer before.

"If you want to hang back and get all religious on us, go ahead," Zach scorned. "But the rest of us are going."

"*Get all religious?*" Piper frowned. "Zach, what's wrong?"

"Will you please cease this mindless communication?" Willard ordered. "We will proceed, and we will proceed now!"

Piper turned from Zach to Willard, equally as surprised. Before she could answer, Willard shook his head in contempt and started off. Zach followed.

But Cody glanced nervously around, refusing to move.

"Let's go, Cody," Zach called over his shoulder.

"I, uh ..." Cody coughed. "I think I'll stay behind. You know, to protect Piper and all."

But it was a lie. Piper could see it in his eyes. If anything, it was the other way around—he was hoping she would protect him. How strange. She'd always known Cody to be brave and courageous.

What was going on?

●

It was time to report to Shadow Man. Monica was grateful her cell phone didn't work underground. She was even more grateful that she had to leave the caves to call in her report. It's not that she didn't like the caves ... she was just terrified by them. Or at least where they led to.

Actually, not *where* they led to, but *who* they led to.

By the time they caught the elevator and went back upstairs, they were all pretty jittery. Of course Bruno was the worst. The big lug was shaking hard.

"Are w-w-we th-th-there yet?"

"Yes, Bruno," Silas sighed. "You can open your eyes now."

"Great. Can I go to the bathroom?"

"As soon as I call Shadow Man." Monica punched in his number on her phone. "He's still in the Hummer with the kid. And with any luck, he's still in a good mood."

Silas frowned. "I didn't know he had good moods."

"Don't be ridiculous," Monica snapped. "Of course he has good moods."

"Really," Silas asked, "like when?"

"Remember that day there was a big earthquake in California and a major hurricane in Florida and all those tornadoes in Kansas? And when that giant typhoon hit Asia?"

Silas nodded. "You're right. I think he might actually have smiled that day. Well, at least a smirk."

Finally the phone on the other end picked up and a voice demanded, *"Ssspeak to me ..."*

"I'm, I'm sorry to disturb you, sir," Monica stammered.

"Your very presssenccce disssturbsss me."

"Yes, well, thank you ... I mean, I'm sorry ... I mean—"

"Sssilenccce!"

Monica gave a nervous swallow. Come to think of it, so did Silas and Bruno.

"Have you found them?" the voice demanded.

"It's just as you suspected," Monica said. "They've returned to the compound in search of the boy. They found the elevator and are heading down into the abyss."

"The abysss?" She could almost hear him smiling on the other end. *"Excccellent. The massster will deal with them ssswiftly."*

Monica gave a sigh of relief. "Then you won't be needing us to go down there, will you, sir?"

The three smiled anxiously at each other, giving a confident thumbs-up over a job well done, until Shadow Man answered:

"You mussst return and retrieve the bodiesss."

"But—"

"GO!" The command blasted through the phone with such force that the speaker crackled.

Their smiles wilted as Monica stared at her phone. "Well ... I guess we have our orders."

"We're n-n-not going back d-d-down there," Bruno said.

"Of course we are," she scolded. "As soon as you go to the bathroom, we're heading into the abyss."

"Ah, actually ..." Silas coughed slightly. "The bathroom part won't be necessary."

"Why not?" Monica demanded.

Instead of answering, he nodded at the growing puddle at Bruno's feet.

●

Mom and Dad wandered through one tunnel after another, shouting. "Piper! Zach!"

But there was no answer. Just their returning echoes.

"We'll never find them," Mom said, doing her best to hide the trembling in her voice.

But Dad heard it. He put his arm around her and said, "We will, dear. I promise you, we will."

"First we lose Elijah." She sniffed. "Now Piper and Zach ..."

"We'll find them," he said. "God has not taken us this far to abandon us now. We'll find them."

She looked down and then nodded.

Dad gave her another hug and, once again, they started calling, "Piper ... Zach ..."

●

Zach and Willard followed the cave deeper and deeper. Willard had demanded that he take the lead, and the further they went, the bossier he got.

Things were even worse for Zach. It was as if all his faith was being sucked away. And the deeper they went, the worse it got, until he no longer trusted God for anything.

Finally, unable to help himself, he blurted out: "We're gonna die. I know it!"

Willard glanced over his shoulder and sneered. "What?"

"God's left us here, and we're all going to die!"

"Shut your trap, Dawkins!"

But Zach couldn't stop. " 'Left us here?' What am I saying? I'm not even sure he exists!"

"Who? What are you talking about?"

"God! I don't know what's happening, but—"

"Look, *I'm* in control here!" Willard barked. "Not God."

"But—"

Willard spun around, raising his flashlight over Zach's head. "You shut up, or it's gonna be lights out for you, got it?"

●

Even though she was far away, Piper heard the sound of Willard's shouting echo through the cave.

"Cody?" She turned to see him huddled against the side wall, wide-eyed and frightened. "Something's going on here. Our thoughts, our feelings—they're getting out of control."

Cody nodded.

"And it's getting worse." She paused, listening to the shouting. "Especially for Zach and Willard."

"What can we do?" Cody's voice was shaking.

For the briefest second, Piper wanted to throw up her hands and tell him to forget it. What did she care? Let them fight their own battles. The same with little Elijah. Then, suddenly, out of the blue, she remembered what Dad had said in the car:

"We're in a battle . . . a spiritual battle."

And she vividly remembered one of the weapons they were to use in that battle.

"Cody." She moved toward him. "There is something we can do."

He looked to her, waiting for more.

"We can pray."

"What?"

"We're not fighting against anything we can see. We're fighting something spiritual. And the only way we can win a spiritual battle is to fight it spiritually."

His eyes were wide as he looked at her. "How . . . how do we do that?"

She kneeled down. "Take my hand. Let's start praying hard. Real hard."

●

Still holding the flashlight, Willard shouted into

Zach's face. "Now get in front of me so I can keep an eye on you!"

"What's wrong with us?" Zach asked. "I don't understand what's happening."

"Now!"

Of course Zach could easily have taken Willard with one hand tied behind his back. Make that two hands. Make that two hands and one foot. But he was worried about the guy. And since God could no longer be trusted to help, it was up to him to do whatever he could. Reluctantly, he took the lead, his faith fading with every step he took.

Together, the boys plunged deeper and deeper into the cave—until suddenly they ran out of steps.

Without warning, the path fell out from under their feet, and the boys tumbled down into darkness. But this fall wasn't like before, when they had all fallen into the elevator. No, this fall seemed to go on . . .

"Aughhhhhhhhhhhhhhhhhhhhhhhhhhhhhhhh!"

. . . forever.

Chapter Ten

The Sword

Zach's cry echoed through the cave so loudly that Piper stopped her prayer. Which was too bad, because the more she prayed, the less selfish she felt and the braver Cody seemed to become. But, even now, when she looked up at him, she saw that same cold fear starting to return to his face.

"What, what do we do?" he stammered.

Of course she was also fighting her own emotions. After all, she wasn't the one who got them into this mess. Wasn't it better just to turn and run away, to save her skin, to look out for herself?

But even as these thoughts filled her mind, she knew they were wrong, and she quickly resumed praying. "Dear God, help me, help us . . ." As she continued, Cody rose to his feet. He swallowed nervously and spoke.

"We've got to ... we've got to go down there and help them."

The words surprised her almost as much as they did him.

"Come on." He reached out his hand. She took it, and they started forward. But they'd only taken a few steps before he started to shake.

"Is it getting bad again?" she asked.

He nodded. "The deeper we go ... the worse I feel."

"Me too."

"It's like something is trying to control my emotions."

Piper nodded. "And if it's doing that to us up here ..." she looked down the tunnel, "imagine what it's doing to Willard and Zach."

Cody gave another shudder.

Piper gripped his hand tighter. "Let's keep praying. Don't pay attention to what you're feeling and just keep walking and praying."

Cody nodded, and they continued.

●

Elijah wasn't sure how long Shadow Man had been gone. They'd been parked along the side of the road for quite a while when the Hummer's door opened and the dark presence slipped into the seat beside him.

"I brought you sssomething," he hissed.

From the sleeves of his cloak, he produced a small cage. Inside was a shiny blue butterfly that flitted back and forth.

Elijah's eyes lit up as he watched.

"You like butterfliesss?" Shadow Man asked.

Elijah gave a shy nod.

Shadow Man lowered his voice. "Do you want to ssssset it free?"

Elijah nodded more enthusiastically.

Shadow Man held the cage before Elijah. At its front was a small door. "Go ahead," he whispered gently. "Open it."

Elijah reached out and unlatched the little door. Carefully, he slipped his hand inside the cage and held out his finger. The butterfly darted back and forth and then, as if knowing Elijah was there to help, it landed softly on his finger.

Elijah smiled as he gently pulled his hand from the cage.

The bright blue wings almost glowed while the butterfly opened and closed them, as if to share its beauty, as if to thank Elijah.

A tiny giggle of joy escaped from the little boy, until Shadow Man's hand appeared and, in one quick movement, crushed the insect.

Elijah's smile turned to horror as Shadow Man tossed the dead butterfly to Elijah's feet. It twitched its wings once, twice, and then stopped moving altogether.

Elijah's big brown eyes welled with tears.

"You loved that little butterfly, didn't you?" Shadow Man hissed.

Elijah nodded. Tears spilled onto his cheeks.

"Remember, I have the power to crusssh everything you love—jussst like that. Do you undersssstand?"

Elijah stared at him.

Shadow Man leaned closer. "Do you underssss-stand?"

Ever so slowly, Elijah began to nod.

"Yesss. Good. Very good. He reached to the Hummer's door and opened it. "I ssshall return in a few minutesss."

He stepped outside and leaned back into the truck. "Think about what I have sssaid, Elijah Dawkinsss. Think very hard." With that he closed the door and disappeared into the dark forest.

Elijah stared down at the butterfly on the floor. Cautiously, he reached down and scooped up the dead creature. He held it in his hands and closed his eyes, silently moving his lips in prayer.

Several moments passed before he looked back into his hands with hopeful expectation.

The butterfly remained dead.

Biting his bottom lip, Elijah placed the creature on the seat beside him. He pulled himself into a little ball, closed his eyes, and began to quietly cry.

He did not see the butterfly begin moving its wing.

•

"Look!" Mom said. "Footprints."

Dad kneeled down to examine the cave's floor. He was already breathing faster in excitement. But only for a moment.

Mom saw his shoulders droop. "What's wrong?" she asked. "They're tracks. Fresh foot tracks."

"Yes," Dad said, slowly rising. "But they're ours. We've been traveling in circles."

It was Mom's turn to wilt. "Oh, Mike ..."

He took her in his arms as she fought back the sobs. "It's okay," he said. "We can't give up. God will do his part. Our part is to believe and keep going."

She nodded and wiped her eyes, doing her best to be brave.

They turned and looked ahead. Directly in front of them were the openings to three tunnels. Without saying a word, they both knew what the other was thinking.

Yes, it was their job to believe and keep going . . . but keep going which way?

●

As Piper and Cody continued deeper into the cave, Piper began whispering the verses her father had mentioned in the car.

"For we wrestle not against flesh and blood . . ."

As she whispered them, her thoughts of selfishness again started to fade.

"But against principalities, against powers, against the rulers of the darkness of this world . . ."

"What are you doing?" Cody asked.

"Bible verses," Piper said.

"Bible verses?"

"Yeah." Remembering more of her parents' conversation, she added, "It's one of our weapons. In fact, the Bible says it's our *sword*."

"Sword?"

She nodded. "The sword of the Spirit."

"I don't get it."

"Me neither," Piper admitted. "But remember the devil took Jesus to the mountain to tempt him?"

"Sort of."

"They didn't use guns or bombs or any of that. Their only weapon was the Bible."

"What's that got to do with us?"

She shrugged. "I don't know, but if it's good enough for Jesus . . ."

Cody finished her thought, " . . . then it's good enough for us. What other verses do you know?"

Piper thought a moment, then recited another:

"I have given you authority to trample on snakes and scorpions and to overcome all the power of the enemy."

"I like that one. Say it again."

"I have given you authority to trample on snakes and scorpions and to overcome the power of the enemy."

"Again."

She did. And each time she said it, she felt a little better. And by the strength returning to Cody's eyes, she could tell he was feeling better too.

Until the darkness passed over them. Not a shadow. But a darkness.

Cody shuddered. "Did you see that?"

Piper nodded. "I wish I hadn't."

It passed again.

She pointed her flashlight to the ceiling, to the walls.

Nothing.

At least nothing she could see. It was more of a sensation. A presence.

"There!" Cody pointed behind her.

She spun around. Again, there was nothing—nothing she could see. But her pounding heart told her something entirely different.

So did the scream she heard in the distance.

●

Dad turned to the left tunnel. "Did you hear that?"

Mom pointed toward it. "It came from that one, there!"

Dad nodded and took her hand. "Let's go!"

Together, they raced into it.

The ground was uneven, and both of them tripped more than once. But every time Mom started to fall, Dad was there to pull her back up. And whenever Dad slipped and lost his balance, Mom was there to help. Together, they went deeper and deeper into the tunnel.

But after several minutes it seemed like they were getting nowhere fast.

"Wait a minute," Dad said, "wait a minute."

They slowed to a stop and caught their breath. They paused to listen but heard nothing. There were no more sounds.

"Are you feeling what I'm feeling?" Dad asked.

Mom hesitated, then nodded. "All creepy and cold?"

"Yeah."

"Like when they kept us prisoners in that cell or dungeon or wherever that awful man was holding us?"

Again Dad nodded. "Exactly."

"What do you think it is?"

Dad shook his head. "I'm not sure. But when we were in the cell, do you remember what we did? It not only made us feel better, but it helped us get out."

Mom looked at him. "Do you think that will work?"

He gave no answer.

"Here," Mom repeated, "do you think that would work here?"

"I think whatever we were battling there is the same evil we're dealing with here."

Mom started to nod. "All right, then, let's give it a shot."

Dad agreed and once again they took each other's hand and continued down the tunnel. Only this time they did more than run. This time they tried something else as well.

Chapter Eleven

The Pit

The scream belonged to Zach—that much she knew. Piper raced through the cave, shouting his name until she ran out of cave ... well, at least cave floor. Suddenly, it dropped before her, revealing a giant cavern stretching far below.

Fortunately, she dug in and was able to stop.

Unfortunately, Cody didn't, which explains why he slammed into her from behind.

"Cody!" She started to fall, but he reached out and grabbed her, pulling her in and holding her close.

Once they'd caught their balance and realized they were hugging, they immediately let go.

"Uh, sorry," he coughed.

"That's uh, that's okay," she stammered.

They looked back to the cavern and inched their way over to the edge. They were standing atop a giant, fifty-foot cliff. Piper shined her flashlight back and forth until she discovered ... down at the bottom ...

"Zach!"

But her brother didn't hear. He was too busy swinging his arms and covering his head—all the time shouting, "No, no! Get away! No!"

She tried again. "Zachary!"

He continued waving his arms like he was fighting off an unseen attacker. But what was it? And where was Willard?

Then she saw it. A misty smoke. It was pouring out of a cave at the far end of the cavern. It blew out of the opening toward Zach and encircled him, swirling slowly around his body. But it wasn't mist. Not entirely. Because the longer she stared, the more she caught glimpses of something else. Wings. Tiny black wings.

"Zach!" she yelled. "Zach, can you hear me?"

At last he looked up and saw his sister. Relief flooded his face as he cried her name. "Piper!"

"What is that stuff?"

"I don't know!" He continued slapping and batting the air. "It's all around! They're everywhere!"

Whatever they were, they weren't good. Piper could tell by the cold chill wrapping around her shoulders and the giant knot in her stomach.

"Zach, something's not right!"

"You think?" Zach replied, still swatting at the shadows.

"We've got to pray!" she shouted. "You've got to join me and Cody in prayer!"

Zach didn't answer. In the shadows, Piper could just make out the frown clouding his handsome feature.

"Zach?"

"Prayer didn't work for Elijah," he said, just barely loud enough for her to hear.

Piper was silent, not knowing how to answer.

"If all that God stuff works, why is he still missing?" Zach continued. "And Mom and Dad—why did they get kidnapped in the first place?"

It was Piper's turn to frown. This didn't sound like Zach at all.

"Why are we here? Why are we lost? Why are—"

"I don't know!" Piper interrupted. "But I know you're being attacked, and I know we've got to pray."

"Pray?" Zach shouted. "To whom?"

"What do you mean, *to whom*? To God!"

"Yeah, right," he scorned. "We don't even know he exists."

Piper couldn't believe her ears ... or her eyes.

For even as he spoke, the shadows surrounding him grew darker and thicker. More and more solid.

More and more powerful.

●

Deep in the caves, Monica slowed and held up her hand for everyone to stop—which, of course, meant Silas banged into her, which, of course, meant Bruno banged into both of them.

After completing her mandatory glare at them, she whispered, "Do you hear that?"

Everyone grew quiet and strained to listen. It was faint, but there was no missing the quiet sound:

knock-knock-knock

knock-knock-knock

"It sounds like a code," Silas said.

"Maybe someone's trapped," Monica exclaimed.

"Maybe it's a monster!" Bruno cried.

knock-knock-knock

knock-knock-knock

"It's louder," Monica said.

"Or closer," Silas whispered.

"We're all gonna die!" Bruno cried.

Monica turned to him and let out a weary sigh. "Bruno ..."

"We're all gonna die and get eaten!"

"Bruno!"

"Or get eaten, then die! Or get eaten, then die, then—"

"Bruno, put a sock in it."

He stopped and looked at her with hurt in his eyes.

Seething in disgust, she shook her head and pointed at his legs.

"What?" he asked.

"It's your knees."

The big fellow looked down to see his knees banging together spastically.

knock-knock-knock

knock-knock-knock

"Oh." Monica blinked in disbelief and turned to continue down the tunnel. Honestly, five more minutes of this and she was really going to lose it.

•

Elijah woke as the Hummer's door opened.

Shadow Man entered. "Ssso, have you given thought to what I have sssaid?"

Elijah simply looked at him.

The dark form moved closer. "Do you not grow weary of people thinking you are a misssfit, sssome sssort of freak?"

82

Elijah was surprised at how easily his thoughts had been read. Truth be told, there were days when he wished he were, well, *normal*.

A flicker of a smile crossed Shadow Man's face. He scooted closer and lowered his voice. "You have powersss that no one around you undersssstandsss. Not your friendsss, not your family. How lonely you mussst feel."

Elijah glanced away. He could feel himself being drawn into the man's powers.

A clawlike hand reached out and turned Elijah's face back to him. "But I undersssstand. I undersssstand you have powersss greater than even you are aware. And if you will join forcesss with my master, there isss nothing we cannot accomplisssh together."

Elijah tried turning his head, but Shadow Man held it firmly. "Propheccciesss can be changed. You need not oppossse usss. Combine your powersss with mine. Join me in ssserving the master, and together we can defeat the enemy."

Elijah tried closing his eyes, to push the thoughts away. But the man's words slithered into his brain. They made such sense. Why fight? It would be so much easier to simply deny God and to give in.

Chapter Twelve

The Battle Rages

"Zach, you've got to pray!"

But her brother did not answer. He didn't even bother looking up.

"Zachary!"

The blackness continued pouring out of the cave and surrounding him—so thick that he could no longer see her. Or hear.

"Zachary!"

She gasped as more of the blackness began taking shape. Besides the wings, she now caught glimpses of faces. But not human faces. More like the creepy, inhuman faces of gargoyles on old cathedrals.

She looked back down to the cave. Was it her imagination or could she see eyes deep inside it? A pair of them. Red and glowing.

She gave an involuntary shudder.

She turned around to Cody. He was pressed against the wall, cowering with his old fear. She could tell that it had returned.

Piper closed her eyes. She just wanted to leave—get away from all this pain and despair. It would be so easy to turn away and leave all of this darkness. None of it was her fault. She hadn't caused any of these problems. It didn't make sense to stay here and suffer.

Stop it! she ordered herself. *This isn't right! I will not give in!* But talking to herself wasn't the solution, and she knew it. So, once again, she closed her eyes and began to pray.

Dear Jesus, I need your help. We've prayed. We've quoted your Word. But there's another weapon. What was it? What did Mom and Dad say? What—

Suddenly, singing filled the air.

Jesus loves me, this I know . . .

Her parents! She spun around. They were approaching. And they were singing!

For the Bible tells me so.

She raced toward them. "Mom! Dad!"

They fell into an embrace as tears filled her eyes. It felt so good to be in their arms, she could stay there forever.

No! She caught herself. It was another form of selfishness. Her brother needed her help, and he needed it now.

She pulled away, motioning to the cavern. "It's Zach! He's down there in some sort of pit. And there are these awful, evil things attacking him and—"

"We know," Dad said. "We could feel something was going on."

"That's why we started singing," Mom explained. "That's why we started worshiping."

"Well, don't stop!" Piper grabbed both of their hands and pulled them toward the cliff. "Whatever you do, don't stop!"

When Mom saw her son surrounded by the evil blackness she cried out, "Zach! Zachary!"

"He can't hear you!" Piper said. "Those things are stopping him."

"What can we do?"

"It's a battle," Piper said. "Just like you taught us. A spiritual battle. I've been praying, I've been quoting Scripture but I forgot to—"

"Worship," Dad completed her thought. "We have to keep singing."

"Right," Piper nodded, "We have to keep worshiping and singing!"

Mom looked down to Zach. She was at a loss for words.

But not Dad. Taking a deep breath, he started singing again:

Jesus loves me this I know . . .

Piper joined in.

For the Bible tells me so.

Mom turned back to them. They nodded for her to join in. And slowly, haltingly, she did:

Little ones to him belong.

We are weak, but he is strong.

Piper paused a moment. Was it her imagination or were those faint screams coming from the cavern? She peered down at the darkness surrounding Zach. The misty faces seemed to be twisting as if in pain, as if something were hurting them. Not only hurting them, but making them grow fainter.

Dad must have seen it too, because he shouted, "Louder. Sing louder!"

And they did:

Yes, Jesus loves me,
Yes, Jesus loves me. . .

The screams grew worse, the cloud thinner.

Suddenly, the air crackled with a roar or a voice or a thought . . . it was hard to tell which. But Piper knew exactly where it came from. She looked down into the black tunnel. The red eyes glowed with rage as the sound roared in her ears:

YOU HAVE NO AUTHORITY HERE!
THIS IS MY DOMAIN!

"Keep singing," Dad shouted. "Keep singing!"

Yes, Jesus loves me,
The Bible tells me so.

"Again!" Dad shouted. "Again!"

And so they repeated the song, singing with more and more confidence, watching as the blackness around Zach's head grew fainter and fainter.

●

"Join usss," Shadow Man repeated as Elijah continued looking deep into his eyes. He tried looking away but could not help himself.

"No more battlesss. No more fighting. The massster will give you all that you desssire."

Shadow Man had him. It was over. Until . . . ever so faintly, he began to hear singing. At first it was barely discernable. But it grew louder and louder. Soon, a tiny smile appeared on his lips.

"What?" Shadow Man demanded. "What are you thinking?"

And then, softly, Elijah began to hum.

"Ssstop that."

The humming grew stronger.

"Ssstop that thisss inssstant!"

Finally, Elijah joined in the song:

Jesus loves me, this I know...

●

Piper was the first to see him ... the old man they had run across so many times since they'd begun their journey. He stood on a ledge across the cavern from them. How he got there, she had no idea. His eyes caught hers and seemed to twinkle.

There was a flash of light, and suddenly he held a giant broadsword. But not a sword of steel. This was a sword of words. The very words she and Cody had quoted from the Bible. Amazing! She could actually see them, right there in the shiny blade of light.

The remaining creatures that circled Zach must have seen them too, because they began shrieking and howling. Then, as if desperate, they rose from Zach and raced toward the man. He swung his sword, effortlessly swatting them away. The creatures screamed as they sailed across the cavern and slammed into the wall, finally sliding to the ground.

The next arrived, and the man swung again, repeating the process ... with the same results.

And then the next ... and the next ...

They came faster and he swung faster until everything was a blur ... the swarming mists of darkness racing at him, the glowing blur of the sword swatting them aside.

"Dear God ..."

Piper looked over to her father, who had once again begun to pray.

"We take authority over this darkness, in the name of Jesus."

At the sound of the name, the man with the sword looked up. For a moment, he seemed to smile. Then, suddenly, he leapt into the air, floating toward the cavern floor. For the briefest of seconds Piper thought she saw wings, but she couldn't be certain.

As he landed, the few dark mists still surrounding Zach pulled away.

"Cody!" Dad motioned to the boy who was still curled up against the wall. "Join us."

Cody hesitated.

"We're not the ones who have to be afraid. Come on!"

He rose to his feet, cautiously glancing from side to side. Finally, he moved to join them as Dad reached out for Piper's and Mom's hands. They were forming a circle. A prayer circle.

But they were one short.

"Zach!" Dad shouted.

Piper looked down into the cavern. The clouds had left Zach and were retreating back to the cave where the red eyes glowed. Already, she could see a difference in her brother's face. It was clearer. Brighter.

"Zach!" Dad repeated.

Zach looked up, for the first time hearing his father's voice. "Dad!"

"We're going to pray. Join us."

"I don't think there's a way to climb up there."

"You don't have to; just pray where you are!"

"Got it!" he shouted.

Piper couldn't tell if Zach could see the man with the sword or not. But she could. And she watched with amazement as he started toward the clouds of blackness that had retreated to the cave's entrance. Their little mouths snarled and snapped as he continued his approach.

"Dear Lord." Dad's voice echoed against the stone walls with authority. "We order the enemy to leave. In your name we command him to go and—"

As Dad continued praying, the man raised his sword. He began swinging it into the clouds. Screams of pain and howls of agony filled the cavern as he continued forward—driving them into the tunnel.

Dad squeezed Piper's hand, and she looked at him. "Don't get distracted," he said. "Our job is to pray."

She nodded and lowered her head as he continued to pray as the creatures continued to scream.

●

"What's that shrieking sound?" Silas asked.

"Ghosts?" Bruno trembled.

"Demons!" Monica shuddered.

"Us getting out of here?" Silas cried.

"YES!" all three screamed as they turned and raced back to the elevator.

●

The screaming slowly faded into faint echoes, which finally ended altogether.

Piper opened her eyes and peeked down into the cavern. The clouds of blackness had disappeared. She knew they had escaped deeper into the cave along with the glowing red eyes. She also knew they were defeated.

At least for now.

And the man with the sword?

He'd also disappeared. Big surprise. But she knew they would see him again. At least when he was needed.

In the silence, she heard someone crying, whimpering. Zach heard it too. She watched as her brother slowly walked over behind a boulder and found Willard curled up in a ball, sobbing.

Zach gently put his hand on the boy's shoulder. "It's okay, Willard," he said. "It's over. It's all over."

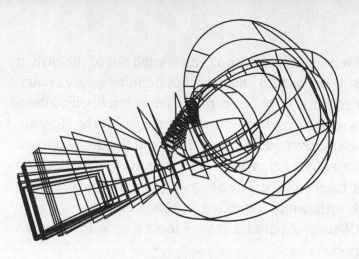

Epilogue

Now that his mind was clear, it didn't take Zach long to start searching for footholds and begin climbing up the steep cliff. Of course he did plenty of slipping and sliding, but eventually he reached the top and joined his family.

It was a little harder for Willard (actually, a lot harder), which was why everybody tied their shirts and coats together to make a type of rope with a sling to help pull him up.

Of course there were more than enough hugs to go around, and Mom cried. To be honest, Zach felt his own eyes burning a little, though he was careful to keep it hidden from everyone. After all, he did have his reputation to keep up.

Eventually, they turned and started out of the cave. It was still just as cold and dark, but definitely not as scary. They traveled for what seemed forever but finally, after a few wrong turns, they found themselves at the elevator. The good news was it still worked and the doors opened for them. The better news was it carried them back up to the creepy office. The best news was they were able to quickly get out of the office and back outside.

"Weird," Zach said as they looked around. "There's still nobody here."

"There was." Willard pointed to some fresh tire tracks. "But they must have left. And by these skid marks, I'd say they were in a major hurry."

Piper smiled. It was nice to hear Willard talking normally again. Granted, he could be kind of odd sometimes. Okay, lots of times. But, let's face it, that oddness was part of what made him so fun.

She turned to her parents and asked, "So what do we do?"

Dad gave a heavy sigh. "I guess we head back through the woods to the RV."

"And then?" Zach asked.

"And then we find Elijah. Come on." He started forward.

But he'd only taken a couple steps before Zach called, "Dad?"

His father stopped. "Yes, son."

"Shouldn't we, you know, like pray or something?"

Dad broke into a smile. "You're right," he chuckled. "You're absolutely right." He turned and headed back to the group. "So ... do you want to lead us?"

"Sounds good to me," Zach said.

Piper couldn't believe her ears. Zach wanting to pray? Amazing.

Then again, maybe it wasn't so amazing. After all, everyone seemed to have gone through some positive changes. Who knows, maybe even Zach was changed a little for the better. All right, *very* little. But, hey, a little change was better than no change.

Once again the family gathered for prayer

"You okay?" Piper asked as Cody joined her side. "You haven't said a word since we left the cavern."

He shrugged. "Guess I'm kind of embarrassed. I mean, nobody likes cowards."

Piper's heart melted a little for him. "It wasn't just you, Cody." She pointed to herself. "Nobody likes self-centered brats either." Then motioning to Willard she added, "Or know-it-all bullies or," she motioned to Zach, "big-time doubters."

"Yeah, but still ..." He dropped off, unsure how to answer.

"We've all got weaknesses," she said. "Whatever was down there was just trying to use them against us. But the important thing is, we discovered how to fight back, how to beat it." She stopped. But when she stole a peek at Cody, she was grateful to see him nodding as if she actually made sense.

"Okay," Zach said, "everybody grab a hand."

Without a word, Cody reached out to take her hand and squeezed it. Suddenly she forgot what she was embarrassed about.

Zach continued. "We're going to pray that we beat these bad guys once and for all."

Cody squeezed her hand a little tighter. She returned it.

"And we're going to pray that we find my little brother.

Everyone nodded. Then the group bowed their heads and began.

●

Elijah heard the flutter of something pass his ears. He opened his eyes to see the butterfly circling his head. He wasn't sure how long he'd been asleep, or how long he had been traveling with Shadow Man. All he knew was that he had needed the rest. Another battle was about to begin, and it would call for all of his strength.

Funny thing about battles. It seemed like every one pushed them to their limits. And just when they were sure they couldn't go another step, they somehow found the strength to take it. And then take another. It was almost like someone was giving them extra strength. Like someone was training them, making them stronger and stronger.

Elijah smiled quietly. Because he knew who that Someone was. And he knew that that Someone would never let them slip through his fingers. Because he loved them. Loved them more than they would ever know.

The butterfly made one last circle before landing on Elijah's shoulder.

The boy smiled just a little bigger and then he started to hum. It was another song of worship.

The Elijah Project

The Chamber of Lies

Bill Myers

bestselling author

The Adventure continues in

The Chamber of Lies

Chapter One

To the Rescue

"That's impossible!"

Willard looked up from the computer in the back of the rattling RV. "What is?" he asked.

"How can Elijah send us a message?" Thirteen-year-old Piper blew the hair out of her eyes. "He doesn't even know how to turn on a computer." She scowled back at the message on the monitor.

Don't try to save me!

Shadow Man has weapons you don't understand.

Elijah

Willard, Piper's geeky inventor friend, shoved up his

glasses with his chubby sausage-like fingers. (Willard liked to eat more than your typical guy — actually, more than your typical *two* guys). "Run it past me again. Who exactly is this Shadow guy?"

"*WHO* isn't the right word," Piper said.

"More like *WHAT*," Zach, her sixteen-year-old brother, exclaimed. "We heard him speak back at Ashley's."

"Heard?" Willard asked, shoving up his glasses again.

"It's a long story, but believe me, the dude is not something you want to mess with."

"Everything all right back there?" Dad called from the driver's seat of the RV.

He and Mom sat up front as they drove through the twisting mountain road. The past few days had been rough on them. First, they'd had to leave the kids behind while they acted as decoys for the bad guys. Then they'd been kidnapped. Then they'd lost little Elijah. Then they'd wandered deep into mysterious caves and a cavern filled with strange supernatural beings. Definitely not good times. In fact, on the fun scale of 1–10 they were somewhere below 0.

But at least they had Piper and Zach, and their two friends, Willard and Cody. Together, the four kids sat at the back table.

"Don't worry about us," Zach called up to his parents, "everything's cool." He shot a look to Piper, telling her to keep quiet about the message on the computer screen. She couldn't have agreed more. After all that Mom and Dad had been through, they didn't need to worry about strange new weapons.

Suddenly, Dad hit the brakes and everyone flew forward.

Piper screamed and nearly hit her head on a cupboard, but Cody reached out and caught her in his arms. As the RV shuddered to a stop, he looked down at her and asked, "Are you okay?" His eyes were worried.

Piper gazed into his incredible blue eyes and half-croaked, "Yeah." She always half-croaked when she looked into his eyes. But it wasn't just his eyes. Everything about him made her a little unsteady on her feet (and a little fluttery in her heart).

Zach called up to Dad. "What's going on?"

"Looks like a detour," Dad said.

A sheriff approached the side door of the RV. Zach rose and opened it for him.

The man stuck his head inside. "Afternoon, folks."

Piper caught her breath. He looked exactly like the homeless person who had helped them in the streets of L.A. . . . and the customer who had helped them in the mountain restaurant . . . and the angel who had fought for them in the cavern.

Piper stole a look to Zach. The way his mouth hung open, she knew he'd noticed it too.

"Is there a problem, Officer?" Dad asked.

The man nodded. "Highway is out. You'll have to turn around."

"But—"

"There's a dirt road about a mile back. It'll take you to where you're going."

Mom frowned. "How do you know where we're—"

"And be careful," he interrupted. "You folks still have plenty of dangers ahead. But you'll be okay. You've got plenty of folks looking out for you."

It was Dad's turn to frown. "I don't understand. 'Plenty of folks?' "

"That's our job," the officer smiled. "To look after the good guys." With that, he stepped back outside … but not before catching Piper's eye and giving her a quick wink.

Piper could only stare. Who was this man? She moved to the window for a better view. But by the time she arrived, he was gone.

●

"They are coming thisss way."

Monica Specter stared across the picnic table to Shadow Man. Looking at the massive bulk of darkness always gave her the creeps. Actually, looking at him didn't give her the creeps, not being able to see him did. Well, at least not *all* of him. There was something strange about the way the man always sucked up light—even in the brightest day.

"Want I should hurt them?" Bruno, her brainless assistant, asked. He sat on the bench beside her. To make his point, he reached into his coat for his gun. A thoughtful gesture, if it hadn't been for the soda can sitting on the table beside him.

The soda can that he knocked over with his elbow.

The soda can that dumped its fizzy contents all over Monica's lap.

She leapt to her feet, wiping the soda away. "You idiot!"

"I'm sorry," he said. For a moment he looked puzzled, wondering if he should help her or use his gun to shoot the offending can.

Shadow Man saved him the trouble. With a wave of his arm, he sent Bruno's gun flying out of his hand and into the side of Monica's parked van. It gave an ominous *THUD* then fell to the ground.

"Your weaponsss are of no ussse," he hissed. "Not in thisss battle."

Monica glanced nervously at her two assistants: Bruno, who was as big as he was stupid, and Silas, who was as skinny as, well, as Bruno was stupid. The three of them had spent many days tracking down Elijah. And now, with the help of Shadow Man, they had finally captured him.

But instead of looking scared, the six-year-old sat on a nearby rock, humming happily to himself. Talk about strange.

Stranger still, Monica had never heard Elijah speak. In fact, she was beginning to wonder if he even knew how.

A low rumble filled the air. A vehicle was coming up the dirt road that they'd parked alongside.

"Is that them?" Silas asked.

Shadow Man grinned. "Yesss. They've come for the boy."

"Shouldn't we do something?" Monica screeched. (She didn't mean to screech; it was just her normal voice). "At least get the brat out of sight."

Shadow Man turned to look at her. At least she thought he was looking at her. It was hard to tell with his eyes always in shadows.

"After the accccident, I ssshall take care of the child. You three will ssstay behind and sssearch for sssurvivorsss."

"Accident?" Bruno said. "I don't see no accident."

"You will." Shadow Man smiled and for the briefest moment Monica thought she saw teeth ... or was it fangs? "You will."

The rumbling grew louder.

Shadow Man turned to Elijah. "Boy. To the vehicle."

Monica watched as Elijah rose and turned toward

Shadow Man's enormous Hummer. The child's legs began walking, but they seemed to move against his will. He tried to stop, but one stiff step followed another until he arrived at the truck.

The driver, a huge bald man who stood guard, opened the back door.

Monica cleared her throat nervously. "Shouldn't we hide too? We're right next to the road, so they're bound to see us."

"There isss no need. The crasssh ssshall prevent it."

"But I don't see no crash," Bruno insisted.

"Watch and be amazzzed ..."

Chapter Two
The Crash

"Dad," Zach called from the back of the RV. "If this is a detour, how come we don't see any other cars? Or detour signs?"

"He's right," Mom agreed. "I've got a weird feeling about this."

Willard motioned to the computer monitor. "Check it out."

Zach looked down and saw the letters to another message appearing on the screen:

Deer coming from right.

Tell Dad to look out his window!

"Dad," Zach called. "Look to your right."

"What?"

"To your right! Look to your right. Now!"

Dad turned just in time to see four deer appear at the side of the road and dart in front of the RV. He cranked the wheel hard, veering to the left, barely missing them but sending the RV into a squealing skid.

●

Shadow Man watched with displeasure as the RV slid across the road, just missing the deer.

He turned to the Hummer and shouted at Elijah, "And you think that will ssstop me?!"

He raised his arm toward the cliff looming to the right over the roadway. Several giant boulders came loose and began to fall, bouncing toward the RV.

●

Zach was too busy fighting to keep his balance in the swerving RV to notice another message forming on the computer screen:

Rocks! Look out!

The first boulder slammed into the vehicle's side. The force was so powerful that it ripped the steering wheel out of Dad's hands. He grabbed it and fought to regain control of the vehicle. For a moment it looked like he had it, but then the second boulder hit. And then the third. And the fourth. The RV was batted around like a ping-pong ball as rocks continued to hit it.

"Hang on!" Dad shouted.

Dishes fell from the cupboard, crashing to the floor.

Everyone was yelling. Zach stumbled, tried to catch himself, and was thrown down.

But only for a second.

Before he realized what was happening, he was thrown into the left wall of the RV—then the roof.

They were rolling!

Bodies flew past him, legs kicking, people screaming. Glass exploded around him. There was more yelling as he hit the opposite wall, then finally the floor again.

Well, not actually the floor. More like Willard.

"Oaff!"

Zach landed on top of him, grateful for all the junk food and extra doughnuts the chubby kid had eaten, cushioning his fall.

"Sorry, Willard."

"That's ... okay ..." the kid groaned.

Zach scrambled back to his feet. He looked around to see if anyone was hurt. And then he saw Dad slumped over the wheel, blood trickling down the back of his head.

That's when he panicked. "Dad!""

●

Monica watched with amazement as the big RV finished rolling and landed back on its wheels, filling the air with dust and smoke.

"Well, don't jussst ssstand there," Shadow Man hissed.

She turned to see the massive bulk of a man stepping into his Hummer.

"Go! Take care of the otherssss!"

Monica wasn't exactly sure what he meant by "take care of," but she could make a good guess. She motioned to Silas and Bruno to follow her toward the RV.

"Grab your gun!" She pointed to Bruno's weapon lying next to her van where Shadow Man had flung it. "Don't forget your gun!"

●

As Piper staggered to her feet, she could hear Zach coughing and shouting, "Dad, are you all right?!"

She called out to her mother. "Mom, you okay?"

"Yes. It's just my leg. It's pinned against the dash, but I'm all right. How's everybody back there?"

Zach was crawling toward the front as Piper glanced to Cody and Willard. They were also rising to their feet. Cody was wincing, holding his right arm, but everyone else seemed okay.

"We're fine!" Piper shouted back.

She glanced around the RV. The kids may have been fine, but the place was a mess — dishes thrown out of the cupboard, everything tossed around and dumped on the floor. It was as bad as Zach's room.

Well, not quite, but close enough.

"How's Dad?" she called?"

"He's unconscious!" Zach shouted.

Piper sucked in her breath.

"It's the TV," Mom cried. "It fell off the shelf and hit the back of his head! Mike? Michael?"

Zach was kneeling beside him. "Dad, can you hear me?"

Piper's heart pounded as she moved forward to join them.

"Dad?"

She heard a groan and saw him move his head.

"He's coming around," Mom said. "Mike, can you hear me? Michael can—"

She was interrupted by the voice of a woman approaching from outside. "Anybody alive in there?"

Piper frowned. She'd heard that voice somewhere. More than once. But where? A second voice joined it.

"Want me to blow off the door?"

"Not yet, you idiot!" the woman screeched. "Try opening it first!"

"Oh, yeah." The man gave a nervous laugh. "Why didn't I think of that?"

Piper had her answer. There was no mistaking the rudeness of the woman—or the lack of intelligence of her assistant. And because of their missing manners (and brain cells) these were not people Piper wanted to meet again.

Zach must have recognized the voices too. "Dad," he said, "Dad, can you turn on the engine? Dad, can you get us out of here?"

But of course Dad couldn't. He was too busy just trying to open his eyes.

"Anybody in there?!" The woman's voice was much closer. Any second she'd open the door.

"Here," Zach said to his father, "let me scoot you over."

"What are you doing?" Mom asked.

He shifted Dad far enough to ease behind the wheel. He turned on the ignition. The motor ground away, but nothing happened. He tried again.

"Zach ..."

He tried a third time, and the engine finally turned over. It wasn't happy about it, but at least it was running. And just in time.

Suddenly, the side door was yanked open, revealing a woman with flaming red hair. Beside her stood the biggest of her assistants. But they only stood there a second before Zach dropped the RV into gear, punched the accelerator, and took off.

"ZACH!" everyone shouted.

Well, everyone but the red-haired woman and her goon. It's hard to shout when you're busy leaping out of an RV doorway so your head doesn't get ripped off.

●

Shadow Man stared out his Hummer's window watching Monica and her bungling assistant start chasing after the RV. Despite dozens of dents, scratches, and broken windows, it still ran. This surprised Shadow Man and for a moment he didn't understand how it was possible.

Unless...

He stole a look at Elijah, who was seated at the back. Was this more of the boy's trickery? He knew the child had powers, but this?

Shadow Man couldn't be sure. All he knew was that the little brat was humming again. He hated it when the boy did that. He could make him stop, of course. But then the child would simply find some other way of trusting and thanking—of praising—the Enemy.

The Enemy. That was the whole reason Shadow Man was in this mess in the first place. The Enemy had finally started his preparation to bring about the end of days. And for some unknown reason he had chosen little Elijah as one of his most important tools in bringing about that end.

Shadow Man's lips curled into a tiny smile. Well, let the Enemy choose whom he would. And let the boy hum away, because very soon the child would turn his back on the Enemy. Very soon Shadow Man would bring Elijah over to his side of the battle, to where the real power lay.

All it would take was a little time in The Chamber. A little time to show the child the wonders and glories that would be his if he would deny the Enemy and follow Shadow Man's master.

Chapter Three

Decoy

"Where are they?" Zach shouted over the sputtering RV. He checked the cracked side mirrors for any sign of Monica or her assistant. "I don't see them!"

Cody called from the back window. "They've turned around. They're running back to their van!"

"Zach, slow down!" Mom cried.

"I will in just a second."

"We'll never get away!" Piper shouted. "Not in this thing. What do we do?"

"Hang on, I've got a plan."

"That's what I'm afraid of," she groaned. Piper always groaned when her big brother had a plan. Mostly because it was impossible to forget some of his more famous plans...

Chamber of Lies

Softcover • ISBN 978-0-310-71196-4

Zach, Piper, and Elijah are reunited with their parents. But when Elijah is lured into the Chamber, he must face the Shadow Man in a battle for his soul. Only heaven can help him now.

Available now at your local bookstore!

The Star-Fighters of Murphy Street Series

By Robert West

Introducing the Star-Fighters of Murphy Street: three unlikely young heroes bound for some of the zaniest escapades you can imagine.

There's a Spaceship in My Tree: Episode I

Softcover • ISBN 978-0-310-71425-5

Newly arrived from California, thirteen-year-old Beamer MacIntyre feels like an alien in this bizarre Midwestern town. Strangest of all is the spaceship-shaped tree house in his yard.

Attack of the Spider Bots: Episode II

Softcover • ISBN 978-0-310-71426-2

Star-Fighters Beamer, Ghoulie, and Scilla follow a strange clanking sound in their cave labyrinth and stumble onto a screaming one-eyed monster that chases them into a huge cavern enclosing a fully animated miniature world.

Escape From the Drooling Octopod! : Episode III

Softcover • ISBN 978-0-310-71427-9

The Star-Fighters, under attack from pink goblins and Molgotha, a drooling giant octopod, must save a girl locked in a "pink palace."

Boys Bible

Hardcover • ISBN 978-0-310-70320-4

Finally, a Bible just for boys! Discover gross and gory Bible stuff. Find out interesting and humorous Bible facts. Apply the Bible to your own life through fun doodles, sketches, and quick responses. Learn how to become more like Jesus mentally, physically, spiritually, and socially. Part of the 2:52 series for boys.

Available now at your local bookstore!

The Ultimate Devo for Boys
Softcover • ISBN 978-0-310-71314-2

Every girl wants to know she's totally unique and special. This Bible says
that with Faithgirlz!™ sparkle! Now girls can grow closer to God as they
discover the journey of a lifetime, in their language, for their world.

NIV Adventure Bible

Softcover • ISBN 978-0-310-71543-6

In this revised edition of the *NIV Adventure Bible*, kids 9-12 will discover the treasure of God's Word. Filled with great adventures and exciting features, the *NIV Adventure Bible* opens a fresh new encounter with Scripture for kids, especially at a time when they are trying to develop their own ideas and opinions independent of their parents.

Available now at your local bookstore!

NIV Adventure Bible Book of Devotions

By Robin Schmitt

Softcover • ISBN 978-0-310-71447-7

Get Ready for Adventure!

Grab your spyglass and compass and set sail for adventure! Like a map that leads to great treasure, the *NIV Adventure Bible Book of Devotions* takes kids on a thrilling, enriching quest. This yearlong devotional is filled with exciting fictional stories about kids finding adventure in the real world. Boys and girls will learn more about God and the Bible, and be inspired to live a life of faith—the greatest adventure of all. Companion to the Adventure Bible, the #1 bestselling Bible for kids.

A Lucy Novel
Written by Nancy Rue

New from Faithgirlz! By bestselling author Nancy Rue.

Lucy Rooney is a feisty, precocious tomboy who questions everything—even God. It's not hard to see why: a horrible accident killed her mother and blinded her father, turning her life upside down. It will take a strong but gentle housekeeper—who insists on Bible study and homework when all Lucy wants to do is play soccer—to show Lucy that there are many ways to become the woman God intends her to be.

Book 1: Lucy Doesn't Wear Pink
ISBN 978-0-310-71450-7

Book 3: Lucy's Perfect Summer
ISBN 978-0-310-71452-1

Book 2: Lucy Out of Bounds
ISBN 978-0-310-71451-4

Book 4: Lucy Finds Her Way
ISBN 978-0-310-71453-8

Available now at your local bookstore!
Visit www.faithgirlz.com, it's the place for girls ages 9-12.

We want to hear from you. Please send your comments about this book to us in care of zreview@zondervan.com. Thank you.